THE
MONSTER
MOB

ANDREA HERTACH

The Monster Mob

By Andrea Hertach

Published by MRL Management

www.andreahertach.com

ISBN: 978-0-9881129-4-0

Cover design by Matthew R. Lawrence Copyright 2012

DEDICATION

For all my students who have shared the thrill of mystery stories with me over many years. Thank you for inspiring me to write about thoughtful, amazing and clever kids.

And, as always, for my husband, Matt, whose unwavering energy, enthusiasm, support and love continue to empower me no matter what life throws at me.

CHAPTER ONE

The man laughed demonically as he swayed the knife back and forth before me. The steel edge glowed menacingly, reflecting the pale moonlight that filtered between the bars of our prison cell.

He laughed again as he saw the look of horror on my face.

"I'll scream," I warned him.

He grinned and said, "Go ahead. They won't come and help you. You're a convicted criminal just like me. They'd be glad if they had one less mouth to feed."

"But I didn't do it," I exclaimed, beads of sweat lining my forehead as I watched the action of his blade.

"That's your story," he replied, coming closer.

I backed away slowly until all I could feel was the cold, damp stone wall behind me.

He smiled and whispered, "What are you going to do now? There's no way out."

I swallowed hard. My throat was bone dry.

He watched me keenly and slowly lowered the knife, touching the edge of the blade to his thumb, drawing a small river of blood which crawled into the palm of his hand.

"Your turn," he said grimly.

I froze in horror.

"Hey, you there!" the guard called, as he turned the key in the lock and opened the door. My opponent swung towards the guard who faced him with a look of surprise.

"That's a great story!" Mrs. McMichael interjected as a classroom full of eighth graders looked on with mingled horror and surprise at Alexandria, the author of the tale.

"But it's not finished," Alex exclaimed.

"We'll have to hear the rest tomorrow," Mrs. McMichael explained. "The class is nearly over and we have a few other activities we need to complete. Let's get to work." The children dutifully pulled out their notebooks and continued assignments from yesterday's English class.

Andrew leaned over to Alexandria and whispered, "I've just gotta know how it ends."

"The man with the knife gets caught by the guard and removed from the cell. The crazy knife guy starts blabbering about all the crimes he'd committed."

"So," returned Andrew.

"So," Alex put in. "So, one of the crimes he talks about is the very crime the innocent man was wrongly imprisoned for."

"So, they free the other guy in the end?"

"Yeah, when they discover he was in the same cell as the guy who actually committed the crime, they let him go."

"Wow!" Andrew exclaimed. "You're a great writer."

"Thanks," Alex said proudly. She snuck a glance at the teacher. "We'd better get to work."

Andrew nodded in agreement.

Everyone worked quietly until:

"Psst," whispered Pete, as he slipped a folded piece of paper onto Andrew's desk.

Andrew quickly glanced at the teacher. She was working at her desk.

He carefully unfolded the paper and read: Meeting at the Fortress. 4:00 sharp. Pass it on.

Andrew refolded it, glanced at Mrs. McMichael and pushed it over to Charlie's desk.

Charlie quickly read it, grinned at Andrew, shoved his chair out from behind him, and strolled casually across the room. He had to deposit the note on Alexandria's desk.

He hummed innocently, slid the note to her and headed towards the teacher's desk.

"May I go to the washroom?"

"Certainly Charlie," she looked up from her papers.

He sauntered out of the room.

Alex read the note. She smiled to herself, and slipped the little paper into the big red school dictionary. She tucked the book under her arm and headed over to the other group.

"Leeanna," she began. "Didn't you need to look up "alliteration?" she asked smoothly.

"Ah, no –" Leeanna returned. "I've already found that one—"

"Here," Alex said forcefully, and held the book out to her. "Use my dictionary," she smiled meaningfully.

Leeanna knew something was up.

"Thanks," she said and opened the dictionary, flipping the pages to where the note lay wedged discreetly.

She looked at Mrs. McMichael who was busy helping Kevin proofread his story. Leeanna quickly read the note, turned and winked at Alex. She winked back.

When the bell rang Andrew grabbed his basketball and athletic bag and headed for the Fortress.

Out in the hall Charlie offered to hold the fountain handle for the pretty girl with the short skirt and the long legs. As she bent down to sip the cool water she spied the gigantic hairy spider Charlie had dropped on the edge of the basin.

She screamed that blood curdling girl scream you hear in cheesy horror films.

"You fat, nerdy, stupid geek," she yelled and ran down the hall.

"Ah, come on," Charlie called after her. "It's fake."

Then he started howling with laughter.

Pete smiled knowingly. "You'll never go to the dance with her if you keep pulling stunts like that," he advised.

"Ah, she's not my type anyway," Charlie shrugged his shoulders. His foot played with the gum wrapper on the floor by the garbage can.

Pete frowned and picked up the wrapper. "Thou shalt not litter," he preached.

"I didn't put it there," Charlie said defensively. "I'm just playing with it."

"Nevertheless," Pete began. "It's our duty to maintain the school's good image."

"Who elected you school President?"

"Hey, that's a great idea. I'll run for student council president," Pete said proudly.

"Well then, you're going to have to ditch that snotty attitude, Pete the Perfect! Catch ya later," he called as he ran down the hall.

Alex came out of the classroom. "Hi Pete," she said. "I'm glad you called a meeting. I had something I wanted to suggest."

"Well, we'll see if we can fit that into the agenda."

Pete was putting on that business face Alex hated.

"Well, we could let me do the talking at the beginning, then we'd be sure to get to my part," Alex suggested smartly.

"We'll see," he said finally and left.

She secured her knapsack on her back and met Leeanna outside the girls' washroom.

10

"Do I look all right?" Leeanna fluffed up her golden hair as she looked around to see who might be watching her.

"Sure," Alex said absentmindedly.

"You didn't even look, Alex," Leeanna sulked. "Do you like my new eyeliner?"

Alex looked closely at Leeanna's outlined bright blue eyes.

"Nice," she said.

"How come you don't wear make-up Alex? You'd look really pretty you know."

"Thanks," Alex smiled. "I just couldn't be bothered I guess. I've got too much else to do," she said simply.

They headed to the Fortress. It was located way at the back of Charlie's yard. It used to be a playhouse but when Charlie's sister got old enough to be interested in boys Charlie petitioned his parents to let him turn it into a place for him and his buddies. They had agreed.

Alex knocked on the door. One. Two. Three. Pause. One. Two.

Pete opened the door.

"Come on in ladies," he smiled.

They sat around their homemade conference table. Alex took off her knapsack and plunked it down. She withdrew from it a crumpled piece of paper.

"Hi Alex," said Andrew as he placed a plate of chocolate chip cookies on the table. He drew a juice container and five cups out of his knapsack.

"It was my turn to bring the treats," he said.

"Chocolate chip cookies rock," said Alex. "Are they your Mom's homemade ones?" she asked hopefully.

"Hey, would I bring substandard goods to a top secret meeting?" Andrew grinned.

Leeanna peered over Alex's shoulder.

"Hi Andrew," she said slowly and sweetly.

"Oh, hi," he said shortly and started to pour the juice into the cups.

"Why didn't you bring pop Andy?" Charlie asked as he came through the clubhouse door.

"Because juice is better for you," Pete interjected.

"Oh brother," mumbled Charlie, but he noticed the juice tasted really good.

"Everyone here?" asked Pete as he sat at the head of the table as though he were surveying the masses of which he was king. He was tall and lanky, sported strawberry

12

blond hair in a short, spiky do, had alert green eyes and a brilliant scientific mind.

Alexandria was tall with bubbly brown eyes and wavy brunette hair which rested on the edge of her shoulders when she didn't wear it in a ponytail. She was a gifted writer who planned to enrich and entertain the world with her prose.

Andrew sported the cool, blond, California surfer dude look and he was into anything athletic, except surfing which he hadn't tried yet because he had not been to California or anywhere else that boasted surfing waves. He spoke fluent French after spending his elementary school years in a French immersion program.

Leeanna radiated the small statured, porcelain skinned, blonde locked, blue eyed beauty of the movie prom queen. However, despite appearances, she had tested out gifted as a young child and spent four years in another school in the gifted program with Alex, Pete and Charlie.

Charlie's tall, slightly overweight football player body type sometimes made him appear awkward and uncertain of himself. His wavy brown hair and brilliant blue eyes gave his face a sense of serenity and his goofy antics disguised his true intelligence.

Alex, Charlie, Leeanna and Pete left the gifted program and joined the regular grade eight class at their local school. Their parents felt it was important for them to function in a world of regular people after spending a good portion of their childhood in an elite program. Andrew's parents had pulled him out of the French immersion program for the same reason.

After several weeks of trying to gain acceptance among their new classmates, Alex decided to approach the other four about forming their own little secret society where they could be themselves and feel accepted. They'd all agreed without hesitation and started meeting in Charlie's old childhood playhouse.

Charlie looked around. "The whole gang's here. You may proceed Mr. President," he smirked.

Pete deliberately ignored him and carried on.

"I called this meeting of the Monster Mob," he began.

"Ah, Pete," Alex put in. "Weren't you going to let me speak first today?"

The others looked at Pete.

"Ah, yes, I guess so. Go ahead Alex."

Alex unfolded her paper and glanced at it quickly.

She cleared her throat dramatically.

"I propose a challenge to the members of our secret society, the Monster Mob. Pete Weppler, Andrew Belvedere, Charlie Clifton, Leeanna Schmidt, I challenge you all to write the spookiest, scariest, most disgusting tale of terror."

The members all looked at each other in confusion.

"What about you?" Andrew asked.

"Oh, I'll write one too of course," said Alex.

"Is this like a contest?" asked Leeanna.

"You bet it is," Alex explained. "The Mob will have one week to write their stories. Then in exactly one week we'll meet again, read our stories to the whole group and decide whose is the scariest!!"

"How will we decide who wins?" Pete wondered.

"We'll take a vote," Alex explained.

"What do I get if I win?" Charlie piped up.

Alex hadn't thought about that.

Andrew jumped in with, "We could all put in a couple bucks to make a prize fund."

"Wow," exclaimed Charlie. "I could go to Party Packagers and get that gruesome mask of the fiend whose face is half eaten away with acid."

15

"Oh, that's charming. I don't see how anyone could resist that," Leeanna joked.

Charlie smiled mischievously. "It's a-m-a-zing!"

"Yeah, I think I just figured out why this club is top secret," Leeanna said sarcastically.

"Why's that?" Alex asked.

"Because it's social suicide to be caught writing stories, outside of school, like its FOR FUN."

Alex grinned and continued. "Okay. It's agreed. We meet here in exactly one week, at 4:00 sharp.

They all rose from the table, formed a fist with one of each of their hands and joined them in the centre.

"The Monster Mob," they whispered as their fists collided in a silent greeting.

A loud knock at the door, followed by an ear piercing scream, froze them all as the five friends stared at each other wide eyed with alarm.

CHAPTER TWO

The door shook with the power of the pounding on the outside. No one moved.

Then there was a teenage girlish giggling audible on the other side of the wooden planks which formed the door to the clubhouse.

"Hey Loser, supper's ready."

Charlie's face transformed from fright to fury.

"Get out of here Ashley!" he yelled at his sister as he hurled himself towards the door. She was sprinting back to the house as he came bolting out after her.

By now the rest of the gang was laughing with relief.

"Never mind her," Alex said soothingly.

"She's so annoying. One of these days I'm going to get her good," Charlie vowed.

Charlie sat slumped in his chair after school the next day. He had been asked to stay in because he had been caught playing basketball with Amanda's lunch using the class garbage can as the hoop. It didn't seem to matter that she was actually finished eating and that he was just chucking around her lunch garbage for fun. Oh well, perhaps the teacher thought he should get a more suitable hobby.

He was busy writing out "How I can use my time more wisely" when Mrs. McMichael said, "Excuse me Charlie, I'm going to leave the room for a minute. I'll be right back."

She shut the door behind her.

It was nearly four o'clock but the sky was already very dark. An early spring thunderstorm was approaching. The thick, grey clouds blocked out the sun and the whole school fell under a blanket of darkness.

Slowly, it began to rain. A few drops pattered against the classroom windows smearing the outside surface. Then it began to rain more heavily, the drops resounding loudly as they bounced off the school roof. In the distance a roll of thunder grumbled. Lightning would soon follow.

As the room darkened and the rain continued, Charlie felt a strange feeling overcome him. He felt suddenly alone in an empty classroom surrounded by a storm. What a great setting for a horror story!

An amused grin etched its way onto his chubby face. He could use the school as the eerie setting for his prize winning monster story!

He pulled out some crinkled up lined paper. It would do for a rough draft. He began:

It was a dark and gloomy evening. The school was abandoned as only the teacher remained at her desk marking papers. She sat alone as the storm brewed outside.

Charlie re-read the last line: "Storm brewed," he said it over and over. That sounded good. He smiled and wrote on.

A heavy wooden door slammed shut at the end of the hall. A clap of thunder echoed across the town. The teacher put her red pen down and shivered. She sensed someone was in the building with her. She knew she was not alone.

The lights flickered and went off.

She held her breath in fear. She was alone in the darkness and someone was waiting.

19

In a soft, shaky voice she called, "Whoever you are, I won't hurt you."

She was scared but tried very hard not to let it show.

"If you need some help, I will try and help you."

Her voice echoed through the long deserted hall.

"Hello," she called.

"Hello," she repeated.

Charlie jumped.

"I said hello a couple of times," Mrs. McMichael began. "But you were a million miles away. What are you writing Charlie?"

He nervously covered his story with the sheet of paper he was supposed to be writing for her.

"Here it is," he blurted, handing her the sheet where he had written his ideas on how to use his time wisely.

She glanced over it in silence and then smiled. "Good job Charlie. Maybe you should add creative writing to that list of how to spend your time wisely."

He shrugged his shoulders and smiled back.

"Good idea," he chuckled.

"Can I see what you're writing Charlie?" she asked nicely.

"Ah, ah..." he stammered, a little embarrassed. "It's not ready yet."

"Oh, ok then. Maybe later then," she added hopefully. "You can go now."

He grabbed his stuff and bolted home. He was soaked through by the time he made it to his house. He tracked mud in the back door.

"Hold it right there Chuckeroni," his mother smirked. "Freeze," she added. "That's it. You are under arrest."

"I give up," he said, grinning.

"Drop everything," she instructed.

Charlie carefully put the basketball on the empty chair and plopped his drenched jacket over it. He put his knapsack on the floor under the chair and took a step forward.

"Stop," she hollered. "Remove the shoes," she directed. Charlie dumped his mud encrusted Nikes on the shoe rack.

"Good," Mrs. Clifton said slowly and carefully as though she was disarming a bomb about to explode. "Now the pants."

He looked at her in horror!

"What?!" he exclaimed in disbelief.

"Drop 'em."

"But Mom," he whined.

"Just do it. They're soaking wet and the mud's up to your knees. I won't look."

She turned her head and covered her eyes.

"Hurry up," she said through her hands.

Charlie hurriedly dropped his jeans to the floor, grabbed his knapsack and bolted up the stairs to his bedroom.

After putting on his other favourite pair of jeans he pulled the story out of his bag.

He grabbed a pen and wrote:

"Hello," the frightened teacher said again.

There was no answer. She found her way in the dark and silently removed her scissors from the pencil jar on her desk, clutching them tightly.

She waited.

22

The rain continued. Thunder clapped and was followed by streaks of lightning. The lights flickered and came on.

She couldn't believe her eyes.

Cramped in a small chair behind a student's desk sat a man. His clothes were dirty and torn. The man appeared to be in his early forties. He looked very sad.

"What are you doing here?" the teacher asked him.

The man did not answer. He just continued to stare ahead as though he didn't even hear her.

"Who are you?" she asked him gently.

"My name is Daniel Matthews." His voice was low and raspy as though he had worn out his vocal chords.

The teacher's eyes grew wide with terror. Daniel Matthews was the teacher she had replaced. Daniel Matthews had been killed over a year ago in a car crash.

"You can't be," she stammered. "You're, you're ..."

"Dead, yes I know," he said dismally.

A flash of lightning illuminated the classroom briefly and the lights flickered and went out. The teacher screamed as she saw the shadow of the dead teacher rise from the chair.

23

"Don't be afraid," he begged her. "I have not come here to hurt you. I need your help."

She blinked, hoping to remove him from her vision, but when she opened her eyes he was still there. She could not make him go away like that.

"I don't have anyone else to turn to," he groaned pitifully. "You did offer to help," he reminded her.

"What can I do to help you?" Her throat was stiff and dry.

The ghost sat down again and began speaking. She found it easier to listen to him when the lights were out because then she didn't have to look at his grey skin and hollow, sad eyes.

"The night I died it was a very stormy night, just as it is tonight. I was driving home and I was very upset. I could hardly see, what with my state of mind and the heavy rain. The windshield wipers didn't seem to move fast enough. I thought only about what the principal had said to me that day, and I didn't see the eighteen-wheeler as it pulled out in front of my car.

"Oh my God," the teacher murmured, imagining the crash.

"It happened so fast, I don't think I remember feeling anything."

"Thank God," the teacher whispered.

"I'm here tonight because I have to set something right and I can't do it alone. I don't have much time. When the lights go on again I'll be gone."

"What can I do?" she asked urgently, her fear dwindling. Slowly she returned the scissors to the jar on her desk.

"I had a student in my history class. He came to me with a very personal problem and asked me not to tell anyone. I never did. But somehow another student discovered the secret and used it against him. She told the principal and the student who trusted me, Joshua Samuels, thinks I betrayed him. I was never able to tell him it wasn't me who told his secret. And now my memory as an honest, caring teacher is destroyed because I was killed that day, crushed beneath the tires of that truck."

"What happened exactly?" the teacher asked urgently, sensing his time was almost up.

"Joshua came to tell me he had managed a sneak peak at the upcoming history exam. He hadn't been paying much attention in class, he'd been away a lot, his notes

were poor and he hadn't really studied. His parents had
been fighting a lot and now they were getting a divorce.
His life was upside down. He needed a good history mark
to have a shot at a scholarship he needed. He didn't want
to cheat, but he was pretty desperate. Then I heard a
strange noise outside my office door. I excused myself and
went to see if anyone was there. There was no sign of
anyone in the hall but I found a small math notebook on the
floor right by the door. It belonged to Emily Watson."

"And that's important because…?"

"She was Josh's ex-girl friend. It had been a bad
break up and many of her friends knew she was out for
revenge."

"Is she the one who told the principal about Josh's
cheating on the history exam?"

"Yes, it's complicated though," Daniel explained.
"He didn't actually go ahead and cheat on the exam. He
came to tell me he planned to cheat. I talked with him for a
long time until he felt calm. We made a plan. I would give
him some good history notes, re-teach some sections he
missed and give him a different version of the history exam
he'd seen ahead of time. This way, with a little support he
could write the exam and succeed on his own without

cheating. He left my office very happy and grateful to be given another chance. His honesty amazed me and I didn't see any reason not to help him out. The problem was Emily went straight to the principal with the news that Josh was cheating without knowing about my plan to help him pass the exam legitimately. The principal called me in to her office after Josh left. I died in the crash and Josh thinks I told the principal he planned to cheat. Please clear my name, please..."

The lights flickered on.

Daniel Matthews had disappeared.

The next day the teacher slipped a note through the locker of Joshua Samuels. It read simply:

Dear Josh,

I can't tell you how I know this but I do. I know this to be true: Mr. Matthews did not betray you. He cared about you and all his students. Emily was the one who told. You know that Mr. Matthews planned to help you; you knew that before you left his office. He kept your secret. If you can find it in your heart to believe in him, his spirit will rest.

27

The letter was not signed.

The teacher never heard from Daniel Matthews again. A few days later Joshua Samuels visited the principal. He spoke to her about establishing a scholarship in Daniels Matthews' name.

"Why do you want to do this?" the principal had asked.

Josh said, "To honour a great teacher and a great friend."

It was done.

CHAPTER THREE

Charlie snickered as he watched Alexandria scribble out the last line she had written.

"My story's already finished," he said proudly.

"Big deal," Alex returned. "Rome wasn't built in a day," she said grumpily. "Mine's going to be a great story, you'll see."

Mrs. McMichael stooped and reminded Alex, "This is quiet working time. People can't write if we don't have a quiet atmosphere in the classroom."

"Sorry," Alex whispered. "I'll be quiet."

"Are you ready to conference with a partner?" the teacher asked.

"No. Not yet. I'm not finished," Alex returned.

"That's fine, whenever you're ready then." She left to help Lindsay get the gum out of her hair as she distributed severe looks to all the suspects in the vicinity.

Alex sat at her desk and looked blankly at her paper. She just had to write a block buster thriller. After all, the challenge had been hers. She would just have to win. Everyone in the Monster Mob knew she wanted to be a writer when she grew up so she had to be good enough to win this little contest.

But it was tremendously difficult getting started when the paper seemed to be staring up at her teasing her to put something on it. Nothing happened. She couldn't think of anything.

Suddenly she realized it was because she had nobody interesting to write about. She must find an interesting and compelling character. If she could invent someone amazing then amazing things could happen to them. Then she would have an awesome story!

After school she sat in the park with her knapsack perched beside her on the bench. She was "people watching" -- looking at everyone who passed her and making notes as fast as her pen would move.

A tall, fat lady in a green dress waddled by with a fuzzy white poodle on the end of a leash. A red haired kid chewing bubble gum and holding a Frisbee under his arm whizzed past. A very tall man wearing a dark gray suit and a serious face was past the bench in two steps. His legs were very long and the briefcase he was carrying swung back and forth at the end of his arm like a long brass pendulum in an antique grandfather clock.

Then she spied a dark haired and bearded man slowly walking along the path by the lake. He stopped every few meters and seemed to think about whether or not he wanted to continue along the path. Then he went a little further. He eyed the ducks at the water's edge very curiously. He looked dirty and scruffy. Alex wondered where he had come from and where he was going. The man left the path and slowly made his way to the edge of the lake. He bent and extended his hand into the cold spring water. The ducks swam cautiously closer inspecting the situation. When they realized he had nothing in his hand to offer them they quacked disappointedly and paddled away. The man looked sad, stretched and walked back to the path.

Alex watched anxiously as he came towards her. They had discussed keeping away from strangers in a program at school and her parents had repeatedly warned her of "stranger danger" and yet here was an unknown mysterious stranger coming straight towards her. She stuffed her books, pencil case and Blue Jays baseball cap into her knapsack as the man sat down on the bench opposite her. Only then did he actually seem to notice her. He stared at her with deep blue, glowing eyes; the kind of eyes that could hypnotize you. The kind of eyes that monsters have on the late night horror movies.

Alex got up and ran.

"Alex what's wrong?" her mother asked as she came running through the back door.

"Nothing Mom," she puffed. She had run all the way from the park without stopping.

She bolted up to her room and turned on her computer. She had found her character. The strange blue eyed man was scary enough to be in a horror story.

"The Tale of Old Mr. Martin," she wrote.

Then she began:

Friday Afternoon:

It was 3:08 as I counted the seconds to dismissal time. It had been a long, hard week. My pals and I were looking forward to a fun filled weekend.

I had not been paying attention to the teacher for some time now and I think she was beginning to notice. She told us over and over how she hated boys that didn't pay attention in class. She caught her breath after a long winded speech about the War of 1812, then shifted her glance and looked straight at me. She was about to scold me for not taking notes when the loud, sharp clang of the bell echoed through the halls. Immediately everyone grabbed their books and began to hurry out. I managed to push myself to the front of the crowd so that she wouldn't have a chance to call me back.

As I long boarded home, I thought of the great weekend that lay ahead. Saturday was Halloween night!

The kitchen door slammed behind me as I came running in. I kicked off my shoes, ran to the refrigerator and selected a juicy, red apple into which I planted my teeth. At that moment the telephone rang.

I picked up the receiver, "Hello."

"Hi, Connor," replied the voice on the other end. "Dude, are ya comin' out tonight?"

"Sure thing," I returned.

After supper, I threw on my favourite Nikes and my orange Hollister hoody and headed out.

"Alexandria," called Mrs. Lawrence. "The phone's for you honey."

Alex was so engrossed in writing her story she hadn't even heard the phone ring. She picked up the portable one sitting on her desk next to the computer.

"Hello."

"Hi Alex." It was Andrew.

"Hey Andrew, what's up?" she returned.

"Oh, I just wanted to see how your story was coming along, that's all."

"You wouldn't be looking for ideas would you?" she teased.

"Who me? No way!" he said with mock innocence.

"I had some trouble with mine too at first," Alex admitted. "But then I found an interesting character to write about and now I'm setting up the events in the story leading up to him showing up on the scene."

"Sounds great!" Andrew said jealously.

"Well I hope so. The story takes place on Halloween night so that should give it an extra spooky atmosphere."

"Sounds cool," Andrew remarked. "Well, I guess I'd better go get started myself."

"We only have five days left," Alex reminded him.

"Yeah, the countdown is on. Bye."

"Bye."

Click.

Click.

Alex put the phone down and looked at her computer screen to review what she had written so far. She did a quick spell check and changed a few words to spice things up.

Now something big has to happen, she thought to herself.

Friday- Late Evening:

I met my buddies down by Leslie's Pond. Our fort was a work of art. The frame was simply two poles leaning against two trees. Large sticks stood upright against the supporting poles to form walls. The roof was a plastic sheet covered with tiny twigs and dried leaves. It could not be seen from the street because it was marvelously camouflaged among the tall trees at the edge of the pond.

At fourteen years of age we considered ourselves much too mature to go out trick or treating so we had planned our own Halloween bash at the fort. Tomorrow would be spent preparing for the party. Tonight we were just having a meeting to decide who we'd invite and what we'd bring.

I saw Tom and Jim come down the path followed by Mike, Jeff and his brother, Greg.

Everyone was in high spirits and eager to get the meeting started. We all gathered around a campfire in front of the fort. It was slowly getting dark.

Tom was in the middle of a suggestion when something stirred in the brackish water of the pond directly behind him. I noticed it first but the others were quickly aware of it. No one was sure what it was. The fish had gone upstream ages ago because the pond carried too little vegetation for fish to survive. I squinted to observe the object in the water. It looked dark and lumpy, kind of like a partly deflated basketball but it appeared to be covered in long, dark, matted hair and I swore I could see two bluish glowing points of light coming from its centre. It was difficult to get a clear view of it because it was covered with drooping seaweed. Then it sank below the surface as mysteriously as it had appeared.

Saturday Morning:

As I lay in bed I suddenly remembered a story our neighbour, old Mr. Martin, told me years ago. He claimed his great grandfather had been shot in the back down by that pond about sixty years ago. His body was never recovered and local legend has it that he still haunts the area. I had always thought the old guy told me that story to freak me out or to keep me away from the pond. I had always disregarded the superstitious old man's words – until now!

Mike phoned.

An hour later our whole gang met in Mike's basement.

"I think we should call the whole thing off," said a panicky Jeff.

"We've been looking forward to this for weeks," Jim whined. "Why should we let some practical joke scare us off?"

And so it was decided after a lengthy debate that we would go ahead with the party after all.

Saturday Night:

The evening started off great. The chips arrived with Jeff and Greg. I brought candy apples, and Tom and Jim brought pop.

I came dressed as a Batman. Jeff and Greg came as Dracula and Frankenstein, Tom and Jim came as Edward and Jacob, and Mike looked imposing as Darth Vader.

We munched awkwardly on chips waiting for the Bride of Frankenstein, Bella and Princess Leia to arrive.

We knew the party could not really start until the girls showed up.

We waited.

And then suddenly things seemed to go wrong. The candle in the pumpkin flickered and went out. The old radio flew onto the ground and the batteries dropped out. Someone screamed. The silhouettes of the leafless trees could faintly be seen against the inky deep blue sky.

I gasped with horror. Twenty feet in front of us was a man hanging from a tree, his lifeless body swaying in the cool autumn breeze.

Then we heard a thud behind us as "Bella" jumped out of the oak tree and landed on the soft leaf covered ground. "Frankenstein's Bride" and "Princess Leia" came out from behind the fort. They were all laughing hysterically.

"Oh, very funny," Tom groaned.

"You should have seen the looks on your faces," Michelle laughed again.

"Very amusing, "Bella", Tom grimaced.

"Okay. We're sorry. I can see you guys didn't find it very funny," Michelle continued.

By now she was pushing the hanging man, a bundle of old clothes stuffed with hay, back and forth in an effort to demonstrate it was just a prop and the whole thing was a joke.

The boys tried to recover their egos as they invited the girls to join them by the fire. The girls brought graham crackers, chocolate and marshmallows.

Michelle grinned. "How about a delicious smores as a peace offering?"

The boys couldn't resist and they all huddled around the fire making smores and telling jokes.

"How did you do the trick with the thing in the water?" Greg asked unexpectedly.

The girls looked puzzled.

"What thing in the water?" Savannah asked.

"Look Princess," Jim persisted. "You can tell us the truth now.

The girls spent twenty minutes telling the boys how they pulled all their pranks but never wavered in their insistence that they had nothing to do with any mysterious creature in the pond.

It has been six months since the night of the Halloween party. The mysterious pond creature has not reappeared. Perhaps some things cannot be explained.

CHAPTER FOUR

Pete played with his pen and stared at the blank paper before him. He knew he needed a great beginning – one that would grab the reader and make him or her interested in reading on. The trouble was, Pete didn't even know what to write about, let alone how to begin. He rested his chin in his hands and thought.

What scares people? He thought about what he'd seen on television and at the movies lately. People seemed thrilled by aliens, the supernatural and psychopathic killers. Special effects people spent a lot of time and money creating squishy, slimy things to gross people out.

He put his pen down and went downstairs into the family room. He turned on the TV and flicked the channels in search of something good. An old black and white movie was playing on an obscure channel. Pete turned up the volume and listened.

The very serious man said to the other man, "He who is bitten by the werewolf but does not die, will himself become a werewolf at the next full moon!" The music resounded ominously and a commercial came on.

Pete turned off the TV and went back up to his room. He began making notes, recording random ideas that popped into his head. Whatever he thought about, he wrote down. Later he would decide what he would use for his story and what ideas he would just abandon.

"Pete," his Mom called. "Are you almost ready for bed?"

"Just a minute," he called.

He quickly wrote:

CHANGE—changing is scary

- main character needs to change

- he needs to be scary and maybe scare others with his appearance

- needs to be afraid of himself and want to find a way to stop the process

- setting: nightfall, silence, black clouds rolling across the sky

Mrs. Weppler peeked in.

"Hi Pete," she said.

"Hi Mom," he returned as he dove on his bed and slid beneath the top sheet.

She eyed the pages on his desk.

"Working on something?" she asked.

"Yeah, just a story."

"What's it about?"

"I dunno yet, I've just got some ideas down."

"That's a good start. I bet you by tomorrow you'll have it all figured out."

"I hope so."

"Good night Pete, have a good sleep."

"Night Mom."

The next morning Pete shuffled thoughtfully into school. He had already been thinking about his story at breakfast and on his walk to school. As he pulled out a fresh sheet of lined paper in English class he knew he felt ready to start his first draft.

Mrs. McMichael repeated her instructions regarding the silent atmosphere that was necessary for good writing, and then the pens began scribbling across the pages. Pete pulled his planning sheet out of his jeans pocket, unfolded it, and smoothed it down. He looked over his ideas and then began:

I froze in fear as the thing came toward me. The lights flashed and as it hovered above me, it made a curious humming noise. I surveyed it carefully, wondering who was inside, and if they would reveal themselves to me. Suddenly, I realized that if they saw me standing here observing their landing on Earth, they might capture me to keep me quiet. The saucer rose higher and ejected a gush of steam. I ran for cover and dove beneath the nearest bush.

I waited.

I waited a long time. And I watched as black clouds rolled lazily across the dark sky. It was very quiet.

At length I crawled out from beneath the safety of the bush. I peered up into the night sky in search of the saucer. There was no sign of it. I pulled my cell phone out of my pocket and used its light to illuminate the ground. I was looking for evidence that would prove the visitation of the saucer. I knew no one would believe me unless I had some solid evidence. Detectives on television were always on the hunt for solid evidence before they busted the crooks.

As the beam from my cell phone illuminated the area I scanned the terrain carefully left and right. Soon the pale light rested on a tiny, glowing object. I walked towards it and carefully held the cell phone's light over the object in wonder. It was a shiny and beautifully polished stone, unlike any stone I had ever seen.

I kicked it gently with my shoe and it rolled over. I bent down and pushed the mysterious stone with a crooked twig. Maybe it did just look like an ordinary stone from planet Earth. Perhaps I was wrong to assume it had fallen from the saucer. This little rock couldn't help me prove my story to the newspapers.

An owl hunting in the night hooted in the distance and suddenly I realized I'd been gone a long time and someone might have begun to worry. On impulse I bent down and grabbed the stone, slipping it into my jacket pocket. I zipped up my jacket and began heading for the house. My fingers touched the odd stone housed in my pocket.

Then I ran home.

I hit my alarm clock to shut it up and rolled over on my pillow blinking the sleep out of my eyes. On my nightstand sat the mysterious stone. I looked at it. It looked different somehow in the morning light. I picked it up and examined it closely. It was pinkish in colour and had a crystal like composition. It reminded me of the granite stone I had seen last month in science class. It no longer

had that strange glow it possessed last night. Now it just
seemed like an ordinary pebble.

I pulled on my jeans and dug a clean T-shirt out of
my dresser drawer and deposited the rock in my jeans
pocket.

"Writing time is now over," Mrs. McMichael
began.

Pete looked up in surprise. He was so absorbed in
writing his story that for him the whole school had
disappeared.

"Please put your writing away. It's time for math,"
the teacher continued.

Everyone began getting ready for math. Pete
reluctantly folded up his sheets and stuffed them into his
homework binder.

"To be continued…" he thought to himself.

Later he wrote…..

The Mysterious Stone: Part 2

I ran to the washroom feeling dizzy and sick. My
stomach churned, my head spun and my hands were sweaty

as they gripped the edge of the toilet bowl. I was going to be sick.

After it was over I went to the office and asked to go home. I must have the flu I told the secretary.

My Mom came to pick me up and soon I was in bed looking at a Batman comic book. I felt better now as I lay in my pajamas with my Star Wars comforter pulled up to my chest.

My Mom brought me dinner in bed.

"Wow! Thanks Mom," I murmured.

"You're welcome," she said. "Feel better."

I gobbled it up and continued reading the comic. Then I thought of the stone.

I flipped back the sheets and grabbed my jeans off the chair. I fumbled through the pockets in search of the mysterious stone. Where was it? Could I have lost it somehow while I was sick in the boys' washroom? Or did it fall out somewhere? I checked the pockets again.

Here it is.

I climbed back into bed and looked at the stone. It fascinated me. I looked at every angle of it, studied every facet, smelled it and put my tongue on it to taste it.

47

For the next few days I carried it with me everywhere. It traveled in my pocket with me all day and at night it rested under my pillow. I didn't tell anyone about it. It was my secret and I alone knew of its existence. I became convinced it was from the alien ship.

Today, for the first time, I became aware that I could read people's minds. During the math test Marilyn Dixon's thoughts came to me so clearly she might as well have been yelling the answers at me.

Needless to say, I did very well on that test.

Dean Edwards gave me a very curious look when I passed him the dictionary in spelling today. You see, he never asked me for it; he had just been thinking, "I'd better look up that word."

I knew the stone was giving me this power. This was undoubtedly true. What I wondered was, what should I do with this power?

I decided that I liked this new found skill. For a brief moment I thought about returning the stone to the ground where I had found it, but I have to admit it was just too irresistible. I could read people's minds!

I told myself I was not afraid.

Three nights later I had a dream. In my dream there was a terrible car crash on the other end of town. Three people died, and one was critically injured. Both vehicles involved were totally destroyed.

The next day when I came home from school Mom asked me if I heard the horrible news.

"What news?" I asked as I slam dunked my basketball into the laundry bin.

Mom gave me a funny look but continued to explain.

"There was a terrible car crash on Queensville Road. Three people were killed and one was—"

"Critical," I interjected.

"Yes," she seemed surprised and then smiled sadly. "So you already heard."

"Yes," I lied and went up to my room.

So now the mysterious stone had given me yet another power – the ability to predict the future. I smiled to myself and rubbed it fondly. I was secretly thrilled and couldn't help but wonder what new power I might get next.

That night I had another dream.

This time my mother put two slices of bread into the toaster and as she pushed them down, the toaster exploded with a shower of electrical sparks. I knew she was dead.

I sprang up in bed and wiped my sweaty forehead with my pajama sleeve. I knew I could stop this. I had the power to prevent this from happening. I threw back the sheets and slid into my slippers. Slowly, noiselessly I crept downstairs to the kitchen. I unplugged the toaster and hid it in the trash can by the back door. Tomorrow I would think of some explanation for the missing toaster.

I went to sleep, smiling in pleasure at the thought of how I had managed to overcome fate.

In the morning nothing happened. We had cereal for breakfast and I went off to school.

Marilyn Dixon came walking along the sidewalk and I knew she was going to trip and fall into the mud puddle around the corner. I could have warned her but I didn't. It was too good to miss old Super Brain going for a splat. I laughed so much it hurt. I just kept rubbing the stone in my pocket as I walked away.

That night I awoke and glanced at my alarm clock. 11:59.

Then its glowing red digits flicked to 12:00. Involuntarily I curled up in bed as a sharp pain ripped through my entire body. I reached up and clicked on my reading lamp as I began to shake, and I grew hot and then cold. My arms and legs ached terribly. I watched helplessly and in horror as my limbs changed shape. They transformed into small, twisted, tree-like appendages. My torso shrank to match them. My skin turned blue and tiny bumps sprouted from the blotchy surface. My head ached and tears flooded my eyes as two finger-like growths pushed their way out of the top of my skull.

I fell off the bed and rolled to the long mirror by the door. I struggled to stand on those misshapen blue legs and strained my neck to see my reflection.

And then I knew I had been given the final power. The mysterious stone had made me like them, and now I was trapped.

Pete smiled as he wrote the last sentence of "The Mysterious Stone."

"This otta win me that prize," he grinned.

CHAPTER FIVE

In science class the next morning Pete sat next to Leeanna. She noticed his self-satisfied, "Aren't I the greatest?" look and asked,

"What's with you Weppler?"

The smile spread across his face.

"I just finished writing the winning story last night, that's what!"

"Oh yeah."

"Yeah," he cleared his throat. "And don't even try to get it out of me. I'm not telling you what it's about ahead of time. You'll have to wait and hear it at the meeting like everyone else."

"Who wants to know?" she said smartly, pretending not to be the least bit curious.

"You do," he returned.

"Do not," she snapped.

"Do too."

"Do not."

"Do too – "

"Would you two please watch what's happening during Matthew's space experiment," said Ms. Watson.

52

The science teacher was looking directly at Pete and Leeanna. Some of the students were looking at them too.

"Sorry Ms. Watson," Pete murmured.

"Yeah, sorry Ma'am," Leeanna offered.

Ms. Watson smiled and turned to Matthew. "You may continue now that we have everyone's attention.

After science class the group filed out into the hall and headed for their lockers. Leeanna followed Pete to his locker.

"So you're really ready for the big meeting," she whispered.

"I told you I was," he returned, looking carefully around to make sure no one was listening to them.

Leeanna smiled coyly, stared intently with her deep blue eyes and whispered, "Won't you give me a teeny little hint about your story?"

"No way," he whispered hoarsely.

"Ah, come on Petey."

"Look Leeanna, batting your eyelashes might work on Andrew, but not on me."

"What do you mean?"

"Leeanna, everyone in the club knows you joined 'cause you think Andrew's hot."

Leeanna drew in a deep, shocked breath and exclaimed, "That's not true!"

"Whatever," Pete said as he slammed his locker door shut and clicked the lock in place.

He started to move away.

"That's a lie Pete," Leeanna followed him.

"I don't care whether it is or not," he said exasperatedly.

She followed him around the corner.

"Who told you that?" she demanded.

"Nobody," he exclaimed. "You can just tell, that's all."

Pete knew he had to be careful to hide his own disappointment because he was the guy who actually liked Leeanna. Andrew never paid any attention to her at all.

"So you think I joined the club just because of Andrew? I bet you think I can't even write a story."

Pete stopped and looked at Leeanna. She was pretty, yes. And well dressed in all the popular brand names. And she could be very sweet. But was she a writer? Pete thought not.

"You're not even answering me, you jerk!"

She was really angry now. "I'll show you, Pete Weppler. I'll write the best story ever and then you'll choke on it!" she exclaimed and ran down the hall.

There was nothing else Pete could add to that disaster.

After finishing her homework that night Leeanna called Alexandria.

"Hi Alex," she said into the telephone.

"Hi Leeanna, how's it going?"

"Rotten. I've been trying to think of something to write for my story but I can't think of anything. I just suck at this."

"Want some help?"

"I thought you'd never ask," she laughed.

"I'll be over in a few minutes," Alex hung up the phone.

The girls spent more than half an hour discussing Leeanna's story possibilities. They considered main characters, their personalities, what problem the characters must solve, where the story is set, how to describe things using the five senses, how to create a mood and keep things action packed. Leeanna did not want to admit to anyone that Pete's lack of confidence in her this afternoon had really rattled her.

When Alexandria left a little while later, Leeanna was ready to tentatively begin:

The Night Crawler

Silently she followed the man in black as he sped through the alley. He headed for the subway. She watched him carefully, giving him just enough space to move without spotting her but not so much that she would lose track of him.

She sat in the same subway car and watched him as she pretended to read a copy of The Toronto Star newspaper. Her reporter's instincts told her he had noticed her. She tried to appear calm.

He got off at Bloor Street and she quickly slipped out the other door. Stopping by a newsstand, she waited until he went around the corner of an old Victorian building. She watched as the young man dressed in black jeans, shirt and jacket disappeared into the night. She scampered after him, her heels making clicking noises on the hard concrete sidewalk.

Following him into the ebony night descending on the gloomy street, she was overcome by the strong smell of pepperoni pizza coming from a nearby shop. It made her stomach growl and her mouth water.

Suddenly a large and powerful hand sealed her mouth shut and a strong, muscular arm wrapped around her body and held her in a vice-like grip.

"Don't fight me, and I won't hurt you," the man whispered harshly.

With unbelievable speed, he whisked her away to an abandoned red brick house. He set her down easily, as though she weighed nothing.

Anxiously, she smoothed her rumpled skirt and blouse and asked shakily, "What do you want with me?"

The man smiled warmly, his green eyes sparkling in the glow of the street lamp. Surveying him carefully, she noticed he was extremely good looking: he was tall and athletic in stature; he had wavy dark hair and an eloquent demeanor that made her think of the aristocratic men from Jane Austen's novels.

"What is it that you want with me?" he returned calmly.

She stared at him questioningly as her fear inexplicably started to diminish.

"You've been following me for quite some time," he observed. "What are you after?"

She looked around awkwardly. He gently took her hand and ushered her into the house. Closing the heavy oak door behind them, he silently led her to an antique leather wing chair. It was carefully positioned next to an ornate marble fireplace situated in the parlor of the nineteenth century house. The fire was burning in the hearth as though they were expected.

He motioned her to sit in the chair.

She sat silently and waited.

"Tell me what you want," he demanded.

"I've seen you – " she blurted.

"What?" he growled softly.

"I saw you kill a man behind a warehouse, and then I watched you bend down to his lifeless body and suck the blood out of him."

The vampire smiled a sad and tired smile.

"Oh, I see," he said softly.

He was silent for some time. She watched him nervously, wondering what he was thinking.

58

At length he asked, *"What do you plan to do about it?"*

"I –I don't know," she stammered. She knew the moment she said this he would know she hadn't told anyone and that she was the only witness. A lump of terror swelled in her throat as she realized this meant all he had to do was kill her and his secret would lie dead with her.

"Do you know who that man was?" the vampire asked.

"No," she murmured.

"He was a drug dealer. He was responsible for several drug related deaths in the downtown area. Some of the victims were kids, too young to understand that the teenage feeling of invincibility does not make them immortal. Drugs are a quick road to death."

"And so you just finished him off?" she asked boldly.

"Trust me, that guy didn't deserve to live."

"It's up to the law to take care of criminals," she countered.

"Oh, really?" he continued. *"And who is taking care of those kids? How many more deaths do you think*

would have occurred before, "the law", would have, as you say, taken care of this slime?"

She was silent.

He was silent.

His eyes glowed intently but she met his gaze with courage.

"I know you think what I'm doing isn't right, that it doesn't meet with civilized society's approval."

How could he know that was what she was about to say?

"But you must understand I am not human. I do not govern my life by human standards or laws. I saw an opportunity to assist your pathetically weak race and I took it. How can you condemn that?"

She was silent again, not knowing what to say.

"I am not above or beneath the law," he continued. "For mankind I do not even exist: I am a myth, a legend, a figment of the supernatural imagination. I am not of your world, but if I see a chance to help, to do something good, I just do it. I am not evil even if history presents me as such."

She looked at his long, lean face. It was pale in the firelight but smooth as marble. She realized in that moment that he didn't appear mean or cruel but rather sad and perhaps lonely.

"I guess I can kind of see your point," she conceded. "I suppose we should be grateful you eliminated a piece of scum like that guy."

He said nothing, looking intently at her.

"Really, I'd like to believe the legal system, justice and all that stuff works, but the truth is that's a load of crap. Some people fall through the cracks. Justice doesn't always prevail."

Suddenly he smiled at her and impulsively took her tiny hand in his.

"Why?" she asked.

"Why what? he repeated, suddenly looking confused. She could feel he was shaking slightly.

"Why do you work to protect us? Wouldn't it be easier and safer to stay invisible? Aren't you risking yourself whenever you make contact with any humans?"

"Keeps me from getting bored," he quipped.

She spontaneously giggled. "So you're telling me that's what vampires do when they get tired of blowing up stuff in video games and there's no new episodes of The Vampire Diaries on TV?"

He grinned. "You're pretty funny for a stuffy old reporter."

She pulled her hand away, only pretending to be angry. "I'm not stuffy and I'm not old. I'm only twenty four."

"Baby," he joked.

"How old are you?"

He took her hand back and wrapped his strong fingers around it.

"I'm going to answer your first question: why do I skulk around trying to help humans? Because I was once weak, frail and imperfect when I was human, but I still had value. The good need help on this planet so they will not be consumed by the evil. For every environmentalist doing something to help stop pollution ten others are busy dumping chemicals and wasting the planet's resources in the pursuit of making money. And so, I secretly assist the good where I can."

"How long has this been going on?"

"Oh, you clever girl. I see this is your way of getting me to tell you how old I am."

She smiled at him and he squeezed her hand gently and reassuringly.

"For generations," he said. Then he smiled again and added, "I prevented the car crash your mother almost had when she was carrying you."

Her eyes grew wide in surprise. His anxious green eyes met hers, looking for approval and possible acceptance.

"You mean to say if you hadn't intervened I would — "

"Not have been born. That's right," he finished.

"Oh, my God!" she gasped.

They were both silent, their eyes and hands locking them together.

"Thank you," she whispered.

"No thanks are necessary," he said simply. "Just make the most of your life. Do good things and continue to help people when you can, just as you did when you wrote that article for the Toronto Star."

"You read the piece I wrote on housing for the elderly?"

"Yes, I did. It was a fine piece of writing and did much to help the cause."

His pride in her work gave her a sudden feeling of intense pleasure. Why was what he thought so important to her?

They were silent again.

He continued to hold her hand.

After some moments she boldly took her other hand and placed it soothingly on top of his.

Abruptly he stood up and held out his arm for her to take.

"Come on, it's time you went home before someone thinks you're missing," he said sensibly as he led her to the door.

"But I know all your secrets," she smiled up at him mischievously.

"Will you keep them?" he asked seriously.

"Your secrets are safe with me," she whispered.

"Thank you," he murmured.

"So you won't have to kill me to keep me quiet," she grinned.

He smiled warmly and as he leaned in closer to her, he whispered, "I have other plans for you."

Then he kissed her.

Leeanna grabbed her phone and called Alexandria.

"Alex," she said breathless with excitement. "I've done it, I wrote the story, and it's great. It has a cliffhanger ending

"Awesome. See you at tomorrow's meeting. I've gotta go now Lee. I have to stop my little brother from blowing up the house with his chemistry set.

Click.

Click.

Leeanna fell back on her bed and gleefully thought about how annoyed Pete Weppler was going to be when he heard her amazing story. It would blow him away.

CHAPTER SIX

The Monster Mob met in the club house and anxiously anticipated the sharing of their stories. The members sat around the table nervously sipping orange juice and crunching granola bars.

Pete began. "OK, Gang. Who's going to go first?"

They all looked at each other.

No one moved.

At last Pete said, "Alright, I'll read mine."

He cleared his throat and began reading The Mysterious Stone.

Everyone was silent and listened carefully. After the final sentence Pete shut his binder.

Andrew exclaimed, "Wow, Pete. That was awesome. Who's going to read next?"

Leeanna piped up. "I will", she said and shot Pete a challenging look.

After hearing The Night Crawler Pete whispered, "That was amazing Leeanna."

"Really?" she returned.

"Yeah, it was really good."

It was easy to see that Leeanna was very pleased at the respect in Pete's voice as he complimented her story.

"Thanks," she murmured, surprised.

"Gee, Pete, maybe you're not such a jerk after all," she joked.

Surprisingly, he smiled back.

Alexandria read The Tale of Old Mr. Martin next and everyone enjoyed it too. The boys' group in the story reminded the gang of their own secret society so Alex's story had hit close to home. What if something spooky like that were to happen to them?

"That was awesome," Charlie exclaimed.

"Thanks," Alex returned smiling. "Let's hear yours now."

"Yeah, champ. Lay it on us," Andrew said encouragingly.

"Alright, alright," Charlie returned, only pretending to be reluctant. He was really very eager to share The Return of Daniel Matthews.

After he finished reading everyone applauded just as they had after each of the other stories.

"That was fantastic Charlie," Alex put in. "Where did you ever get the idea?"

Charlie explained his experience the day he had had the detention and was stuck in the school when the storm started.

"This creeped out feeling came over me, and I knew it would be a great setting for a ghost story. Then I just let my imagination run wild until I thought of something scary- you know- like a good nightmare."

"Yeah," Leeanna added. "What could be worse than the ghost of a teacher? The living ones haunt us kids enough as it is."

Everyone started laughing.

"What about yours Andrew?" Pete asked.

"Yeah Andrew," Charlie reminded him. "Yours is the last one. Let's hear it."

Andrew pulled a few crumpled sheets of paper out of his knapsack. He smoothed them down with nervous hands.

"Sorry gang, this is actually my first draft. I had ball practice last night so I didn't spell check it or anything."

"Disqualified," Charlie joked.

"No way," Leeanna said forcefully. "No one said spelling counts.

Alex broke in, "Cool it you guys. Let's just hear the story."

Andrew began:

Adam blinked his eyelids rapidly in an effort to focus his vision. Soon he could see the empty white ceiling above him. Stiffly he turned his neck and glanced at his surroundings. There were shelves of books and bottles and test tubes and beakers and solutions all crowded into the room that housed the cot he was lying on.

A large dark eyed man entered the room and stared down at him, a huge grin spreading across the man's face.

"You're awake," he said simply.

Adam found his voice and said hoarsely, "Where am I?"

The man pulled a battered old chair next to Adam's cot and sat down beside him. He cleared his throat purposefully and began.

"Hello Adam. I'm Dr. Noah. The things I'm going to tell you are going to be difficult for you to fully comprehend because they are so fantastic and unbelievable."

Adam's eyes grew wide.

"You are at the Science Centre," the dark eyed man continued. "You have been here resting for two hundred and seven years."

Adam struggled awkwardly to rise from the cot but the man gently pushed him down.

"You haven't the strength yet Adam. Just rest easy and let me tell you all you'll need to know."

Adam was silent. His eyes darted around the room not recognizing anything. He was breathing rapidly and wondering whether or not he should trust this man. Did he have a choice?

"Over two hundred years ago you were dying of a rare disease. So, in an effort to save your life, your family decided to have you preserved, so to speak, until a cure to your illness could be found."

"My family," Adam murmured.

"You don't remember them do you?"

"I don't think so," he answered hesitantly.

"That's OK Adam. Perhaps it will be less painful for you not to remember them. You need to realize they're all gone now."

"Gone!" Adam blurted.

"That's a great story!" Leeanna interrupted.

"Shh," Alex whispered.

"Read on," Charlie added.

"Alright everybody, just shut it so we can actually hear Andrew's story."

Andrew, pleased with everyone's enthusiasm, grinned and read on:

"Rest now Adam. I'm going to get you something to eat."

Dr. Noah effortlessly removed some strange looking devices from Adam's arms and legs and rapidly left the room. The door clicked shut behind him. Adam made a sudden and brief attempt to get up from the cot but fatigue overcame him and he unexpectedly fell asleep.

After some time Adam awoke and found himself alone.

On the table next to him he saw a pile of old books. He sat up and eagerly began examining the antique books Dr. Noah must have left for him. They were leather bound in lovely shades of red, green and brown and must have been very old. Adam glanced at the titles: A Tale of Two Cities, Oliver Twist, A Christmas Carol.

71

Dr. Noah entered.

"Nice aren't they?" he asked as he observed Adam's admiration of the books. "They're all first editions of novels by Charles Dickens."

"Yeah, they're pretty cool," Adam returned. "They have a funny smell."

Dr. Noah grinned. "That's the smell of history meeting science."

Adam looked puzzled.

"That's actually the smell of paper and ink decaying over time. With high resolution photography we have been able to preserve the look of an ancient document but eventually the original will crumble into bits."

"That kind of sucks."

"Tell me about it," Dr. Noah chuckled at Adam's response. "I've spent my whole career trying to keep things from falling apart."

He quickly changed the subject. "I have some information about your family that you really ought to know."

Adam put the book down and looked intently at Dr. Noah.

"I thought you said it would be better if I didn't know anything about my family."

Dr. Noah lowered his voice. "I think it's important that you know that your origins reach back to Dickens, THE great nineteenth century novelist."

Adam regarded the books on the table with surprise.

"Wow," he murmured incredulously.

"You obviously have a brain worth preserving," Dr. Noah exclaimed.

"How old am I?" Adam wondered.

"Your data card stated you were eighteen at the time of your preservation so that makes you two hundred and twenty five years old," he grinned.

Dr. Noah pulled a small mirror out of the pocket of his lab coat.

Adam studied his face carefully. He had soft brown slightly wavy hair that flowed neatly from a high brow. He had intense blue eyes and a charming smile.

"That's me," he said softly. "I didn't even remember what I looked like."

"That's OK. You haven't looked in a mirror for over two hundred years."

73

"Yeah, well I guess I haven't really done much of anything for a couple hundred years."

Dr. Noah smiled warmly.

"Listen Adam," he began. "There are some people who want to see you."

"What?" Adam was suddenly flustered. "Who?"

"Reporters, historians, scientists, to name a few."

"Why?" Adam interrupted.

"Because, you're unique Adam. A scientific marvel. You've made history. You are the first successful human revival. I succeeded in bringing you back even though the scientific community spent the last two hundred years thinking it was impossible, or at least improbable."

"I think I just want to be left alone," Adam said quietly.

"I know," Dr. Noah said soothingly. "But it won't take long."

In the weeks that followed it became clear that Dr. Noah had been wrong when he reassuringly told Adam he could soon go on with his life. Reporters and photographers were in his face constantly, interviews didn't stop and the visits continued.

One wall of his room at the Science Centre was made of plexiglass. It had been installed so that visitors to the Centre could observe Adam as he watched TV, read or ate his meals. He was the wonder boy, the phenomenon. The whole world knew of his amazing existence by now and came to watch him as though he were a monkey at the zoo.

"How long is this going to go on?" he yelled at Dr. Noah one afternoon. "I feel like a freak in a circus side show. I can't stand this anymore. I have no privacy, no friends, no fun, no life. What was the point of giving me back my life if I can't live it?"

"I understand you're upset Adam – "

"Upset doesn't even cover it. I feel like a prisoner here in my little habitat," he said in frustration. "There must be a law against forcefully keeping me here or are we living in France in the seventeen hundreds?"

"I see you've been reading A Tale of Two Cities," Dr. Noah said proudly.

"Well there's not much else to do around here!"

"Look Adam, I'm sorry. We have no choice. It cost a great deal to keep you for two hundred years. We have to make some money –"

"Oh, I see it now," Adam returned disdainfully. "I'm a Science Centre money maker. I'm such a valuable commodity that you guys are never going to let me out of here are you?"

"Now Adam," the doctor said calmly.

"Are you?" Adam yelled.

There was a painful silence between them.

At last Adam remarked, "This can't be what my family intended when they agreed to this process, or I think they would have let me die naturally.

He slumped into his chair and closed his eyes. "Now I wish they had," he murmured.

As Dr. Noah quietly left the room he heard Adam mumble, "Sydney Carton found a way to get Charles Darnay out of prison."

"Why doesn't he just run away?" Leeanna interrupted.

"That can't be so easy. I would think the security was pretty heavy duty and how would he survive in a world that progressed two hundred years beyond his birth?" Pete said.

"Consider that he has no identification, no place to go to, no money, if money even exists two hundred years from now and no skills or job he could get ,"Andrew added.

Leeanna looked dismayed. "What did he mean about Sydney Carton getting Charles Darnay out of prison?"

"Oh, I know this book. I saw the movie one night last week. My mom loves classics so sometimes I get stuck watching them," Alex grinned. "That's from A Tale of Two Cities. It takes place during the French Revolution in the seventeen hundreds. The poor ordinary people who were tired of suffering at the hands of the French aristocracy and nobility rebelled against the system and the entire country was turned upside down as nobles, anyone that even worked for them and even the king and queen were executed. It was unbelievably horrible and many innocent people died. In Dickens' novel Charles Darnay, an Englishman is imprisoned in France and slated for execution by guillotine because he has noble connections. He is a good man and is innocent of any crimes against anyone. It is clear to Sydney Carton that Darnay's death would bring a great deal of pain to his family, especially to

Lucy, the woman both Charles and Sydney love. So Sydney, who looks remarkably like Darnay, decides to work his way into the prison, drugs Darnay so he can't object, switches places with Darnay and has him smuggled out of the prison back to England and freedom."

Alex took a deep breath after that long explanation.

"What happens to Sydney?" Charlie asked.

"He dies in his place and goes in peace because he feels he has done something honourable and good at last," Alex answered. "He is Charles Dickens' most tragic hero, I think."

"Ah, guys, do you think we could just let Andrew tell us the rest of the story?" Charlie urged.

"OK, OK," Leeanna and Pete said simultaneously and smiled at each other.

Andrew read on:

Adam switched the television channels restlessly. TV had not really changed much in two hundred years. Movies and shows were still about people and the troubles they encountered but the commercials were wild. They advertised things Adam had never seen before. The latest trend in kids bikes included navigational equipment, solar

powered engines and something that looked like
retractable wings.

The news came on.

An attractive female newscaster said, "The
Kennedy Shuttle Foundation is searching for suitable
candidates to take the next shuttle to Mars...."

Adam sat up abruptly.

"... with the intention of becoming a colonist.
Many blocks of Discovery City are prepared to sustain
human life and the Foundation is now ready to begin
colonization. If you think you are bold enough to become a
pioneer to this new world, get in touch with the
Foundation."

Website information ran across the top of the
screen.

"The weather today.."

Adam turned off the television.

He could have a future on a new planet. He might
have a chance at a real life if he left Earth. There was
nothing for him here, no reason or person who was dear to
him to make him want to stay. But the real problem was –
how was he going to get there?

After several hours Dr. Noah returned and Adam told him of his plan to become a Martian colonist. Adam knew there was no way for his plan to succeed unless he took the doctor into his confidence.

Adam waited breathlessly as Dr. Noah carefully reflected on the idea.

"Will you help me?" Adam blurted. There was a pleading tone in his voice despite his attempted bravery.

"I have a lot to lose," Dr. Noah said at length.

"I know you do," Adam admitted solemnly. "But I have my life to lose. Look at me here! I haven't even been outside since I 'woke up.' I never would have asked you to risk yourself if I wasn't desperate."

"I know, Adam. You're a good, decent young man. I know you deserve better than what you're getting here. Give me some time to think about how I'm going to handle this. Perhaps when we earn enough money they'll release you willingly and we won't have to fight."

"How much is enough money? And what if they don't want to release me—ever?" Adam stammered.

"Just leave it with me," Dr. Noah said softly. "I'll see what I can do."

And so Adam waited.

Each day the news announced the shuttle program.

The day of the take off approached.

Adam waited.

There were still places to be filled on the shuttle, but Dr. Noah would not commit himself to any specific decisions.

And so, Adam had no choice but to continue to wait.

Impatiently.

Then it was announced.

The shuttle was leaving tomorrow, and Adam knew he would not be on it.

Dr. Noah had not been to visit him in several days, and Adam knew it was because he did not want to face him.

The shuttle was departing in four hours.

Adam curled up on his bed and put his head under the pillow so that no Science Centre tourist could look through the glass and see that he was crying.

After awhile the visitors stopped and it was clear the Centre had closed. His tear stained face felt sticky and hot. He dropped the pillow on the floor and fumbled in his night table drawer for a magazine.

The shuttle was departing in one hour.

He turned the pages of the surfing magazine absentmindedly. His eyes were cloudy with teardrops but he didn't resist letting them roll down his face. He wiped them away and turned another page.

He dropped the magazine as Dr. Noah entered the room. He was red-faced, out of breath and very nervous.

"Come on Adam," he said urgently. "Get up. Get this jacket on," he directed, handing Adam a light spring jacket.

"We've got to move quickly," he added, and grabbing the boy's wrist he pulled him into the hall.

Adam knew not to slow things down by asking questions. In a few moments they were in Dr. Noah's flight mobile and heading rapidly for the sky way.

Adam sat silently overwhelmed at his first sight of the outside world in over two hundred years. Everything moved so fast.

"Where are we going?" he mumbled at last.

"The launch pad," Noah returned. "We have less than an hour to get you on board that shuttle."

"You – " Adam began thankfully.

"Shh," Noah directed. "Let me concentrate."

Adam obeyed. He couldn't quite believe that Dr. Noah had come through in the end.

"Thanks," Adam said simply.

Dr. Noah smiled and said, "Don't mention it."

Then the doctor grinned and said, "Name a street after me in the new colony will ya?"

Adam smiled in return.

"I'll see what I can do," he returned warmly.

Dr. Noah had used his considerable connections to procure the necessary documents and pass cards to admit Adam to the shuttle. In a few whirlwind moments they stood before an official looking attendant who held out her hands to collect Adam's documentation.

"Bye, kid," Dr. Noah said in a fatherly tone. "Have a nice life."

"What about you?" Adam was worried.

"Don't worry about me Adam. I'll take the heat if I have to."

"Why don't you come to Mars too? I'm sure they could use a top notch scientist like you."

"I'm needed here Adam. But who knows? Maybe you'll see me out there yet. Get going now."

He motioned Adam to the waiting attendant who was smiling encouragingly at him.

The two men shook hands.

"Good luck Adam," the doctor said.

"Thanks for everything," Adam returned.

The doctor pressed a little burgundy leather bound book into his hand. It was an antique copy of *A Tale of Two Cities*.

"What's this for --?" Adam began.

"Something to remember me by. You might like to entertain your fellow colonists by reading it aloud. It's a long trip."

"Thanks," Adam smiled and tucked the book into his pocket. "Maybe I'll write a book myself about my experiences as a Martian colonist."

Adam paused and added, "I could call it *A Tale of Two Planets*."

Dr. Noah laughed joyfully.

"That's a great idea."

Adam looked observantly at the attendant. She was tall, elegant, despite the scientific uniform she was wearing, had lovely shoulder length strawberry blonde hair, a radiant smile and sparkling green eyes.

Adam followed her to the metal door on the other side of the hallway and as he turned to take one last grateful look at Dr. Noah, he smiled mischievously and mouthed the words, "She's hot."

Dr. Noah grinned and walked away, knowing that Adam would find happiness in his new life.

Andrew put the paper down.

"Wow!" exclaimed Alex. "You should write a sequel to that one!"

"Yeah, you could tell about Adam's adventures on Mars," Charlie put in.

"Hmm, a sequel to Ahead in Time. I should definitely think about that."

"Wouldn't it be fun if a partner worked on it with you?" Alex suggested.

Andrew laughed. "Yeah. I could use a good writer like you to help me with the sequel."

Alex blushed.

Charlie snickered.

"Smooth move Andy," he said.

"Shut it," Andrew remarked slamming his book shut.

Alex tried quickly to shift the focus of the discussion by saying, "How are we going to evaluate these stories and decide which one's the winner?"

They all looked at one another in silence.

"Let's take a vote," Pete suggested.

"What d'ya think Alex?" Charlie asked. "This whole story contest was your idea. How do you want to settle it?"

"Ah, I don't know guys. It's too hard to decide. They're all such good stories. I don't see how we can choose just one."

"I agree," Leeanna remarked.

"They are all really good," Charlie admitted.

"How are we going to reach a decision then?" Andrew wondered.

"Let's say they all win!" Alex exclaimed.

Everyone looked at her in surprise.

"Are you serious?" Charlie asked.

"Yes, I am," she said hesitantly. "Why hurt anyone's feelings? They're all good stories so why put a label on "the best"? After all, I bet we couldn't decide on a winner even if we had a vote because the stories are all so completely different. Different people's tastes would probably mean we couldn't all decide on the same one."

"But we only need a 3-2 vote with five of us here," Pete reminded her.

Alex was silent, unsure how to proceed. Then she had an idea. She rummaged through her bag and pulled out an empty binder.

"What do you guys say to putting all our stories in here and making a collection, a kind of anthology of stories written by the club members?"

They looked at one another again, and wondered who would be the first to speak for or against Alex's suggestion.

Andrew spoke up first.

"I think it's a great idea," he said as he gave Pete and Charlie a sideways glance to stifle any stupid comments or silly faces.

"Yeah, me too," Charlie added.

"I love it," said an enthusiastic Leeanna.

"I guess we all agree then," Pete stated.

They handed their stories to Alexandria and she began placing them into the binder.

"I'll make out a table of contents tonight," she said.

Above the clubhouse thunder roared and a flash of lightning revealed to them how much time had passed since their meeting had begun.

"Oh, it's late," Leeanna said nervously. "I'll probably be grounded," she whimpered.

The rain let loose and pattered heavily on the well sealed roof of the clubhouse.

"It's pouring," Pete announced as he looked out the window. "If we leave now we'll be soaked to the skin by the time we get home."

"Yeah," Charlie said dismally. "And my Mom will make me take off my -- "

He stopped just in time.

"Sorry, I forgot. We have ladies present." He grinned.

"Ah Chuckster," Andrew said, putting his arm around the shoulders of his good buddy. "You always know just the right things to say."

"Come on Andy, give me a break."

"Sure buddy. Right arm or left?"

"Ha! Ha! Not funny. Do you have any idea how old that stupid joke is?" Charlie returned.

"Well, I'm pretty old," Andrew returned slyly. "I can show you my fangs but then, you know, I'd be forced to kill you."

A clap of thunder silenced the laughter that would have followed Andy's remark.

The lights flickered and went out.

CHAPTER SEVEN

"Oh, great," Pete said with irritation.

"I wish we had left earlier," Leeanna moaned.

"That's what happens when Dads are nice enough to put electricity in play houses. We'd have noticed it getting darker outside if we hadn't turned on the lights," Alex remarked.

A low mournful howl could be heard in the distance.

"I – is- is that a wolf?" Leeanna murmured.

"Naw," said Pete. "It's only a dog in somebody's back yard."

"It sounded like a wolf to me," Charlie added.

"Get outta here Charlie," Andrew exclaimed. "You're letting that spooky story writing go to your head."

"I'm not kidding," Charlie said nervously.

"Neither am I," Andrew said firmly. "Now quit scaring the girls."

"I'm not scared," Alex informed them.

"Neither am I," Leeanna lied.

The rain continued to fall heavily, thunder roared and lightning flashed. The Monster Mob was huddled together around the table trying to decide what to do.

"I just heard something outside," Charlie whispered urgently.

"What?" Pete asked.

"I dunno exactly. It sounds like someone coming up the steps."

Everyone froze and strained to listen beyond the sounds of rain and thunder. Then faintly the sound of footsteps slowly traveled up the steps to the clubhouse door.

They came closer.

Closer.

Closer.

They were large heavy sounding footsteps.

"Hey, in there. You kids, open up!" yelled a gruff man's voice.

He pounded a strong fist on the door.

"I said open up. I know you're in there."

A clap of thunder vibrated through the clubhouse and the kids held hands in frozen fear.

"What should we do?" Alex whispered.

Everyone looked to Pete. Their faces were strangely illuminated by the lightning bursts.

"I dunno!" he blurted. "Don't look at me this time."

"I'm going to have to bust this door down if you don't open it," the monster called.

"Oh my God," Leeanna yelped.

"Don't worry, it'll be Ok," Pete managed to reassure her.

Suddenly the footsteps retreated and then came ahead quickly. With a thud the monster rammed himself against the door. The kids scrambled out of their seats and made a protective huddle in one corner of the room with Charlie and Andrew, the strongest, on the outside. Pete tried to keep Leeanna calm, and Alex curiously peeked out to see what was going on.

The monster pounded heavily on the door. He was determined to break it down and get at the kids, that much was certain.

The door cracked.

Leeanna screamed.

Charlie yelled.

The monster fell through the doorway.

Thunder clapped.

Lightning flashed.

And then –

Silence.

The uniformed man collected himself off the floor, dusted himself off and shone his flashlight at the kids. As he stood the children saw to their surprise and relief that he was no fiendish, child eating monster, but a police officer.

"Okay you kids," he began. "You gave your parents quite a scare by disappearing like that. And why did you make me break that door down? Now I have to take my uniform to the cleaners," he said as he brushed off the remains of a granola bar he had crushed into his shirt.

"Come with me," he directed.

Pete spoke up. "Let us see your badge first officer."

"Good thinking," Leeanna whispered. "We'd better make sure he is who he says he is."

The officer grinned and pulled out his badge.

"Alright kids, I can agree to that. That's playing it safe."

"I think this guy is Ok," Andrew said, looking closely at the badge. "My Dad's badge looks just like this one.

The officer took his identification back and said, "Ok kids, let's get you home."

"I'm going to be in so much trouble if people see a cop in my backyard," Charlie groaned.

"I'll probably be grounded," Leeanna sighed.

"Will they allow you visitors?" Pete whispered.

"I'll ask," she giggled.

"Move ahead Romeo," Andrew joked. "Hey Charlie, don't trip over the door –"

Charlie hit the floor.

" – step," Andrew finished.

Everybody laughed.

"I knew that was there," he said sheepishly. "I just thought I'd throw in some comic relief."

He brushed himself off as he left the clubhouse wondering who had called the police to find them.

It was raining gently now as the low sorrowful howl of a distant animal reached their ears.

"What's that?" Leeanna asked nervously.

"Aah, probably just a werewolf," Charlie stated simply.

The girls looked at each other, their eyes growing wide in amazement.

CHAPTER EIGHT

Okay, so it wasn't a werewolf after all.

Over the next few weeks the rest of term came to an end fairly uneventfully after the night of the Monster Mob story extravaganza and all five of them graduated with all the pomp and circumstance due to such an auspicious occasion.

The birds woke Alexandria with their twittering good morning song, but she didn't mind. It was still early and the sun hadn't even come around to her side of the house yet, but as she rubbed the sleep from her eyes she could see the sky was a soft blue and the trees in the backyard swayed in the lazy breeze. She smiled happily as she spied a robin sitting on the cedar hedge which encircled their back yard. I feel as free as you do, she thought. It was the first day of summer holidays. Two months of freedom lay ahead before the dawn of high school.

Alex slid into a pair of shorts and a T-shirt and made her way downstairs to the kitchen. She put a piece of bread into the toaster and searched the fridge for peanut butter and grandma's strawberry jam. She poured herself a big glass of orange juice and rattled the vitamin container to see if there were any left. There were a few dancing around the bottom. She swallowed one and left one out for her mother.

Alex was thirteen going on twenty-one. She knew her own mind and had her own style. She wore her brown hair loose most of the time although it was almost shoulder length, and she preferred jeans and sport shirts to the designer clothes most of her friends wore. She liked doing her own thing and decided a long time ago it was better to celebrate being yourself than attempting to be a fake copy of somebody else.

"So what are you up to today?" her mother asked as she entered the kitchen and poured herself a cup of coffee.

"Well I thought I'd clean my bike, ride to the store and get a Mars Bar, visit Leeanna, see what the guys are up to, maybe play a little tennis, write a new story –"

"Wow, is that all?" Mom joked.

Alex smiled and said, "I guess I am trying to cram all the good stuff into the first day, but when you've been imprisoned in school for ten months you kind of go crazy on your first day out of the place."

"Alexandria, is that how you feel about school, like it's a prison?"

"Sorry Mom," Alex grinned.

"That's alright. Actually teachers feel pretty much the same way sometimes. I know after ten months with the same group, helping them learn and grow and get along with others, I feel pretty drained and I'm grateful to be doing something different in the summer. I'm working on a book about how to teach kids by using the arts."

Alex gave her mom a mock yawn.

"Very funny, Alex. It's supposed to make school more fun."

"Oh, fun is good," Alex grinned. "Speaking of summer plans and fun, I'd like to talk to you and Dad about going to summer camp. All my friends are going and I really, really, really want to go too. Please, please, please," Alex smiled like an angel.

Her mother slowly sipped her coffee.

"I need you to babysit your brother this summer. I have meetings to go to and this writing to do, your father's working until we take our holiday time with you later in the summer and Jason's only eleven. He'll get into all kinds of disasters if we leave him on his own. Need I remind you about the chemistry set fiasco?"

"Okay, fair enough. I get that you would like to come home to a house that is still standing and not a smoldering heap of rubble, but I need a life and all my best friends are going to this cool camp up north."

"Sorry Alex."

Alex rubbed her temples with nervous fingers. She had to think of something.

Her mother headed to the fridge to get a yogurt.

"Wait, Mom. I have an idea. Let's consider the money you would have paid me to babysit Jason."

"Ok, I'm listening."

"We take that money and put it towards the summer camp fee."

"I'm not following," her mother looked confused.

"We take the money you would have paid me to look after Jason and use it to send him to summer camp and I use my saved up babysitting money from this spring to pay for me to go to camp. This way I get to go to camp and Jason gets supervision at the same time."

"I didn't know either of you would be interested in summer camp," Mrs. Lawrence mused.

Oh no, thought Alex. There was the problem she hadn't thought of: would Jason even agree to go? Probably not, especially if he knew it meant so much to her. She would have to handle this very carefully.

"I'll talk to your father about this and I'll get back to you, okay honey."

Alex slumped back in her chair. She was beginning to have a very bad feeling in the pit of her stomach.

CHAPTER NINE

Charlie opened the front door and was surprised to see Alexandria standing there.

"Hi Charlie," she said glumly. "Do you mind if I come in?"

"Naw," he returned. "But let's go around back. My creepy sister is in the living room tying up the phone talking to her --" he paused and screwed up his face as though he'd just bitten into something sour, "boyfriend," he said disgustedly.

"I figured it was something like that because I tried to call before I came."

"Yeah, we're going to have to have a second line installed for Goldilocks if this keeps up," he quipped.

"Hey, that's a great idea," Alex returned excitedly. "Your second line could be the Monster Mob line and that would make your house the Monster Mob Headquarters."

Charlie sighed. "I don't think so. Besides I don't know how much longer this is going to be my house."

"What are you talking about?" Alex asked in confusion as Charlie opened that back gate and they entered the yard.

"Nothing," he returned quickly. "Anyway Alex, now that it's summer holidays do you think anyone will want to continue the Monster Mob?"

"Well of course they will," she exclaimed. "The Monster Mob is not just a club you know. It's a group of people who are best friends, who would do anything for each other. I know it didn't actually start that way. We kind of just met because we liked the idea of having a secret club, and then we had the spooky story contest and now I think you guys are all like my best friends."

Charlie smiled. "Yeah I guess you're right," he admitted.

"You know I am," Alex confirmed. She put a steady hand on his shoulder. "Now I know something's wrong," she said slowly. "What did you mean by that comment you made about the house?"

"Nothing," he stated.

"Why don't I believe you? You're always the joker Charlie, the comedian. But I think I can tell when you're serious. You could try talking to me."

Charlie looked at her sadly and suddenly felt at a loss for words. His tall hulky frame, chubby face and enormous sense of humour usually left people thinking

101

nothing could upset him. He was surprised to realize Alex understood there was more to him than met the eye. That was comforting and terrifying at the same time.

"Well," Charlie began tentatively.

"Hey Chuck," his sister yelled out the kitchen window.

"What d'ya want?" he yelled back.

"Your creepy friend Andrew is here and don't you go hollering at me," she nagged.

"Thanks Broom Hilda," he yelled sarcastically.

"Kiss my – " she snapped back and slammed the kitchen window shut before they could hear her last word.

"What's her problem?" Andrew snickered as he came through the gate and joined them in the back yard.

Together Alex and Charlie said, "BOYFRIEND," looked at each other in surprise and began to laugh.

"Man I feel sorry for you. Having a sister has got to be tough enough, but having a sister with a boyfriend has got to be deadly," Andrew grinned.

Charlie slumped his plump body into a lawn chair. "Yeah, it's rough man," he admitted with dignity.

"What did you come over for?" he asked suddenly.

Alex regarded him knowingly. He was trying to change the subject from what they had been talking about before Andrew arrived.

Andrew began. "I have this fabulous story to tell you guys. I just saw the movie version of it last night."

"I'm touched," Charlie smiled sweetly. "Andy came over to tell me a story."

"Actually, I went over to Alex's house first but her mother told me she was over here," he grinned.

"Wow man, I'm hurt," he sniffed. "So I was your second choice."

"Sorry dude," he turned and smiled at Alex.

She felt a sudden horror as she knew her face was turning red with embarrassment.

"Well tell us this amazing story," she said quickly to turn the attention away from herself.

Andrew grabbed a lawn chair and sat opposite Charlie. Alex quickly did the same.

Andrew cleared his throat dramatically and began:

On a quiet moonlit night an old man sat on the river's edge and playfully dangled his feet in the clear cool water. He took a drink from a dark bottle and stared at the

103

moon. The trees swayed in the breeze. Suddenly the trees parted and a murderer leaped at the powerless old man. His scream for help was choked out by the murderous fiend who picked him up as though he were no more than a puppet, brutally snapped his neck and threw his lifeless body into the river.

The next morning the police found the man whom they at first mistook for a heap of rags floating in the river. It made newspaper headlines all over the city although the man's identity remained a mystery.

The next day a curious old lady and her daughter entered the bank and withdrew four thousand francs, (that's French money, by the way this story is set in Paris, France) and the bank manager called in a handsome young man named Mr. Le Bon to escort the two ladies to their home with this large sum of money. Mr. Le Bon saw that the two ladies arrived home safely with their money and kindly said good evening to them.

The sun went down and the clouds disappeared to reveal a glowing moon. Everyone had gone to bed except for the two rich ladies who sat up counting their gold coins in their richly furnished room up on the fourth floor on a street in Paris named the Rue Morgue.

Suddenly they heard a strange sound outside and as they turned to look, a murderous creature flew through the window and attacked them. Their screams were heard all over the neighbourhood and many people came out of their houses to see what they could do to help. Behind a brave policeman a few townspeople headed towards the big house. The officer entered the yard and led them up three flights of stairs to the fourth floor. The screams stopped and then there was silence.

When they entered the room, it was clear that everything had been thrown around the room and there was blood everywhere. Later the policeman found the old lady's body outside on the ground, her head in the bushes. The chief of police found the razor that the murderer had used to do this ghastly deed. The young lady, the daughter, had been squeezed to death and stuffed up the chimney.

Alex threw her hand to her mouth and gasped.

"Awesome!" Charlie exclaimed.

Andrew continued in a soft and subdued voice.

The police searched everywhere to discover how the murderer entered and how he left the building, but they could find nothing. All the windows were nailed shut and the only door in the room led to the flight of stairs which the policeman had used and he had not seen anyone escape by that route. The most confusing thing was that all the money was lying all over the floor bespattered by blood apparently untouched. Robbery did not seem to be the motive for this heinous crime.

Andrew absentmindedly glanced at his watch. "Oh, guys, I've gotta go. I've got soccer practice," he announced.

"Wait a minute buddy," Alex exclaimed. "You can't leave us hanging like that. That's not fair."

Andrew grinned.

"Okay, I'll quickly tell you the ending. This famous inspector Dupin discovers a sailor who admits that in his travels he picked up a large wild ape and brought this animal back on the ship. The ape accidentally escaped from his cabin and the sailor has been trying to find him because he knew the animal could be dangerous. In the end Inspector Dupin proves that the ape climbed up a lightning rod, jumped in the window, killed the two ladies and escaped out the window before anyone saw him. The mysteriously nailed shut window, upon closer examination, proved to be able to open and close because it had a secret catch, and the nail only appeared to hold the window shut because it was actually broken and could be pulled out. Naturally, this smart detective helped to capture the killer ape in the end.

"Naturally," Alex said sarcastically. "That is the most outrageous thing I've ever heard. That is totally unbelievable."

"Who wrote that craziness?" Charlie joked.

"One of the greatest mystery writers of all time," Andrew explained. "The Murders in the Rue Morgue was written over a hundred years ago by an American writer named Edgar Allen Poe."

"Demented," said Charlie.

"Seriously," Alex laughed.

"I have to go now," Andrew rose from his chair to leave. "Can I walk you home Alex?"

"Sure."

After they left Charlie wondered how he would be feeling if he had told Alex what was really bothering him.

CHAPTER TEN

They were boarding the bus for summer camp. Leeanna looked around anxiously for Alex but couldn't see her anywhere.

She spied Pete over by the bus, no doubt instructing the driver on something or other she thought humorously.

"Hey Pete," she snuck up behind him.

"What?" he jumped.

"Follow me," Leeanna directed. "I think the bus driver can handle things on her own."

"What do you want now?" he asked in a sulky voice.

"Have you seen Alex? I haven't seen her anywhere."

Pete looked around quickly and then said simply, "No, I haven't. I didn't think she was going to be allowed to go. I thought her parents needed her home to babysit her brother."

He absentmindedly looked at his map of northern Ontario. "We'd better get on the bus."

"I thought Alex had a plan to talk her parents into letting her go," Leeanna sounded desperate.

"I don't know," Pete remarked.

"What do you mean? Alex always has a plan."

"Look Leeanna," Pete advised. "You might as well get that worried look off your face because there's nothing you can do either way. It's up to her parents."

"Oh, God. It would absolutely bite if she didn't come."

Charlie lumbered up to meet them.

"Hey guys. How's it going?" he asked in a friendly voice.

"Hey Charlie," Pete returned as they bumped their knuckles in greeting. "See ya on the bus."

"Why do you look so worried Leeanna?" Charlie asked. "Is this your first time away from home or something?"

"Ha! Ha! Very funny. I'm worried Alex isn't coming."

"Hey there's Andrew. Hey Andrew!" he yelled and waved.

Andrew threw his Adidas bag over his shoulder and hurried over to his friends.

"Hey guys. We're off to summer camp! Can you believe it?" He sounded really excited.

109

"Do you know if Alex is coming or not?" Leeanna grabbed Andrew by the arm.

"How should I know?" he said, quickly pulling his arm away.

"Aaaahhh!!!" Leeanna screamed. "There she is!"

She ran over to meet a smiling Alexandria.

Leeanna practically dragged Alex over to the waiting friends.

"Here she is!" Leeanna announced.

"I can't believe I made it," Alex smiled widely. "I thought for sure the folks were going to stick me with babysitting."

"What happened?" Charlie asked.

Alex pointed at a group of younger students saying last minute goodbyes to parents.

"Jason," Leeanna smirked. "Jason's coming with?"

"That's the only way I could negotiate my way out of babysitting. My parents were cool with us both going to summer camp. They think it's cute." Alex made mock gagging sounds.

"Ah man, he's a pain in the butt," Leeanna admitted.

"Don't worry Alex," Charlie said soothingly. "We'll help you keep him in line."

"I wouldn't have taken Jason for the camping type," Andrew remarked thoughtfully.

"He's so not," Alex admitted. "He almost wrecked the whole thing by refusing to come."

"How did you get him to agree?" Charlie wondered.

"I told him there'd be a lot of hot, older girls here."

The boys exploded with laughter.

"Oh great," Leeanna moaned.

"Don't worry, you're safe. He thinks you're seriously annoying."

The boys continued to snicker.

"Gee thanks Alex," Leeanna returned.

"Just trying to make you feel better," Alex added.

"Gee thanks," Leeanna repeated.

"Hey guys, get on the bus," Pete yelled. Seeing Alex, he smiled and waved them forward. "Gee, I thought Leeanna was going to have a break down when she thought you weren't coming," he said as Alex entered the bus.

Charlie leaned over to Alex and said, "It's great you made it. Now the whole Monster Mob is together."

Alex smiled gratefully back at him.

"Let's get a seat away from Pete the Perfect," Leeanna whispered to Alex.

The engine started and after the driver went through the standard safety speech she turned the key in the ignition and the bus was on its way.

Alex leaned back in her seat not quite believing she was actually on her way to summer camp in Muskoka for three whole weeks. She looked out the window as they got on the highway. Leeanna had already managed to dig her compact mirror out of her purse and was checking her make-up.

Alex grinned.

"What?"

"Really Leeanna. Three weeks of camp and you're worrying about make-up," Alex smirked.

"My mother says a lady must always look her best," Leeanna quoted.

"You don't have to look like a model at summer camp."

Leeanna gave her a shocked look and then whispered, "There are going to be men there."

Alex burst out laughing.

"Shhhh!" Leeanna pleaded.

Alex forced herself to stop laughing. "Don't worry," she said pretending to be serious. "There aren't any men on this bus."

Leeanna gave her a cold glare. "You think you're very funny don't you? One day you'll be sorry. One day the man of your dreams will appear on the scene and you won't be prepared."

Alex thought about that for a moment and then said, "Leeanna, the man of my dreams will have to like me the way I am."

"Hey Alex," Andrew tapped her on the shoulder from the seat behind. "This bus ride is getting boring. Let's say we spice it up a little," he suggested with a mischievous smirk on his face.

"What did you have in mind?"

"You don't happen to have a stink bomb?"

"Andrew!"

"Kidding. We could put Leeanna's make-up on Jason and give him a make over," Andrew schemed.

"Tempting, but not gonna happen," Alex informed him, thinking of her parents' reaction to such an event.

"Do you have another spooky story like that Edgar Allen Poe nightmare?" she asked.

113

"Naw," Andrew returned.

Alex sat up. "I have an idea. You know that game called telephone where everyone in the game just keeps adding something and passing it on?"

"Yeah."

"Well we could do that but make a story out of it."

"What do you mean?" Leeanna asked.

Alex cleared her throat. "I'll start.

It was a dark and story night. The full moon shone its light upon the house where the little boy was ---"

Alex paused and Leeanna and Andrew looked at her in confusion.

"Who wants to continue the story?"

"Okay, I will," Andrew said.

"Where the little boy was making a green and purple goopy potion in the secret room in his basement. Suddenly he heard his mother coming down the stairs. Step. Step. Step. Closer she came and closer. Then suddenly --- "

Leeanna continued.

*"Suddenly the door flew open and the mother
yelled, "What are you doing son?" And he looked at her
and explained, "I'm making a potion Mom. I'm going to
feed it to my budgie so it will become big and strong and
together we will rule the universe."*

Andrew and Alex laughed.

Leeanna stopped and scowled. "I hate how you
guys always act like I'm an idiot," she said harshly.

"No, it's great," Andrew put in. "Go on."

"Alright," Leeanna said softly, taking that as an
apology.

*"So the mother said, "That's nice dear. Have fun
playing." She left the room.*

*The little boy stirred and stirred the potion until he
thought he had the correct thickness. Then he went to the
bird cage and slowly poured the magic potion into its little
water dish. The bird cocked his head from side to side in
confusion. The boy watched anxiously as the little bird slid
its beak into the curiously coloured water and drank it all*

115

up. Then after a few moments of waiting and watching the bird –"

"Bit it," Charlie put in. He had shoved the book he was reading into his knapsack and since he was sitting next to Andrew he decided to join the game.

Everyone laughed.

"Oh smart," Leeanna returned. "Why don't you tell the rest of the story since you just killed the bird."

Charlie froze and looked imploringly at Alex.

"She's right," Alex admitted. "It's your turn to make something up."

"Okay," Charlie began.

"The bird fell to the bottom of the cage and lay there motionless for some time. The little boy started to cry because he was sure he had killed his best friend. Then miraculously, the bird began to wriggle, slowly at first, then more rapidly until it was shaking uncontrollably and making curious noises. Suddenly, it began to grow. It grew and grew until it popped its cage. The boy grabbed the bird and ran outside into the back yard and carried the quickly growing bird to a secluded, tree covered part of the yard. It

continued to grow steadily until its beak reached the height
of the tallest tree which the boy knew was more than ten
meters tall. The gigantic winged creature looked down at
the little boy with death in his eyes."

"Ooh, that's awesome! Who wants to carry on?"
Alex asked.

And that's when the bus engine died.

CHAPTER ELEVEN

"What's going on? Leeanna wondered.

The bus driver radioed for back up and Mr. Evans, the camp councilor, got up from his seat and addressed the campers.

"Okay everyone, let's just relax. There seems to be a little problem with the bus. Just talk to your friends and we'll update you as soon as we can."

He sat down again and waited for the driver to finish on the radio.

"So what happens to the huge bird?" Andrew asked.

The four of them looked at each other, each waiting for one of the others to continue the story while they waited.

The driver whispered something to Mr. Evans and he got up again to talk to everyone.

"Okay everybody, sorry for the inconvenience but the bus is going to need a little repair. There should be another bus along in about a little while so all we have to do is relax and get on that bus when it arrives."

Everyone started pulling out their cell phones and iPods, popped ear buds in and started listening to music, playing a game or calling a friend.

After a few moments of trying to place a call Charlie closed his cell phone.

"What's up?" Alex asked him.

"The service sucks out here," he grunted.

"Who were you trying to call?" she added.

"My mom," he said quietly.

"How come?" she wondered.

"No big deal, I just wanted to make sure she's okay."

"Why would you think she wasn't okay?" Alex asked softly.

Charlie looked like he wanted to say something to Alex but Leeanna and Andrew were staring intently at him so he joked, "Well, she does have to put up with Ashley you know."

"Oh, yeah," Andrew rolled his eyes. "She is a piece of work. You have my condolences bro."

"Thanks dude," Charlie returned. He looked out the window to avoid Alex who was looking so intently at him it was like she was trying to read his mind against his will.

119

Pete waved at the four friends as he asked Mr. Evans if he was allowed outside.

"Ah, Mr. Evans, I think some of us are going to need to use the facilities while we wait, if you know what I mean."

Mr. Evans addressed the campers once again.

"Okay everyone, since we have to wait awhile for the replacement bus to arrive, we're going to let you go outside and stretch your legs. If you need to go to the washroom I'm afraid this is Survivorman style out here and you'll have to find a tree or bush to do your business. We do need you to have a buddy to make sure you don't get lost. Stay close to the bus. There's no need to go very far."

Some of the campers got off the bus.

Alex saw Leeanna walk off with Andrew while she went to check on Jason. He was having the time of his life kicking a soccer ball around with a few friends in a little clearing by the bus.

She noticed Charlie walk a few paces away from the bus heading towards a clump of trees. It looked like he wanted to be alone.

Leeanna was flirting shamelessly with Andrew, complimenting him on his new Under Armor T-shirt and shorts and giggling at whatever he was saying to her.

Alex followed Charlie. She saw him go down the ravine behind another barrier of trees and forest vegetation.

"Charlie," she whispered to the clump of trees and shrubs that she thought concealed him.

His surprised face appeared from behind one of the trees.

"Alex! Are you okay?"

He rushed forward to meet her, jamming his cell phone in his pocket.

"I'm fine Charlie. Actually I was worried about you. Still no luck reaching your mother?"

"Naw. Why would you be worried about me?"

"Charlie, we've known each other a long time and I think we know each other pretty well. I think something is bothering you and you'd like to talk to someone about it. You just don't seem to know whether it's me you want to talk to. You can trust me you know, I'll do whatever I can to help."

"I know Alex. You're awesome. You're smart, funny and beautiful and I –"

"Shhh," Alex whispered urgently. "Do you hear that?"

They were both silent, Alex intently listening for something, Charlie looking anxiously at her for an explanation.

Then in the distance they both heard it: a moaning sound as though someone was in terrible pain. Both of them looked around the ravine trying to locate the source of the sound and then they saw it. On the crest of the hill above them a figure came into view. It was dressed in rags that were torn and stained in places. It limped and held its body in a strangely contorted position as though standing straight was painful. As it moved forward and its undulating gait brought it closer they could see its face was a disease filled greenish hue and its eyes were white and lifeless.

Charlie grabbed Alex by the hand and they ran. They skidded further down the ravine dislodging rocks and mosses as they staggered to find a hiding spot.

After a few moments it was clear they didn't know which way to run or what to do. They did not let go of each other's hands as they looked around at the forest surrounding them.

"Oh my God," Charlie exclaimed. "There's a little cabin over there!"

Without a moment's hesitation they ran for it.

They ran breathlessly up the rickety old steps, threw the old wooden door open, slammed it shut behind them and slid to the floor, their backs against the door.

They were still holding hands.

"Alex, you're bleeding," Charlie announced. He let go of her hand to take a tissue out of his pocket. Gently he wiped the blood off her cheek.

She grinned at him. "I think an evergreen smacked me in the face while I was running for my life."

Charlie grinned back.

"Seriously, Charlie, what the hell was that?"

"I have no idea," he returned. "I can tell you what I think it looked like, but that's not freaking possible."

"What do you think it looked like?" she said slowly.

"You're going to make me say it, aren't you?"

"Yep."

"Okay, that thing looked like a zombie."

Alex looked at him solemnly. "Do you have any idea how crazy that sounds?"

"Sure do. Tell me you don't think the same thing?"

"Oh God Charlie, it can't actually be a zombie. This is not one of our crazy stories. This is real."

They were silent, Charlie listening for sounds that might be coming from outside the cabin and Alex trying to think of a plan to get them back to the bus.

"I'm not exactly sure where we are," Alex admitted.

"Yeah, that would be a problem. The other problem is that we don't know where that zombie is."

"Do you have cell service here?"

Charlie checked. "Naw, nothing. I guess Evans wasn't kidding when he said it was like Survivorman out here."

"Well, we kind of came down a hill to get here. Maybe we should make our way up the hill and we might find the bus."

"Okay," Charlie agreed.

He stood up and looked out one of the cabin's windows. Everything seemed quiet and peaceful. Some birds were twittering in the tree tops.

"Okay, it looks quiet. Let's go," Charlie suggested.

They headed for the door and opened it slowly. Carefully they made their way down the steps, Charlie in front of Alex as though he was ready to protect her should anything appear. Stealthily they walked away from the cabin and turned right to begin to make their way up the incline towards where they thought the bus was. That was when they saw them.

On the hill below the cabin ten, twenty, thirty zombies appeared lumbering up the hill, moaning, groaning, arms extended and waving back and forth as though they were blindly searching for something.

Alex and Charlie were surrounded by zombies in broad daylight with no one to help them, no cell service and for the first time she could ever remember, Alex had no plan.

Instinctively Alex slipped her hand in Charlie's, looked up at him and whispered, "This is not good."

Charlie smiled down at her.

"We're faster than they are," he whispered.

"What?" she blurted.

"Run!!!"

They ran, slipped and dragged themselves up that hill, not once looking back at the zombies they knew must be chasing them. In blind hope they ran towards the crest of the hill, praying they would find the bus waiting for them. They could hear the eerie moaning at their heels.

At the top of the hill, sheltered by some tall pines, stood the bus. People were talking, laughing and milling around oblivious to the zombies' imminent attack.

Alex and Charlie started screaming. "Get on the bus! Everybody get on the bus, NOW. The zombies are coming!"

Everyone turned their heads and looked at them in surprise.

"You're kidding right?" someone said.

"That's a good one!" another person added.

"Nice try," someone else added.

"This isn't a joke," Alex screamed.

"It's true," Charlie yelled. "Get on the damn bus!"

"What's going on?" Mr. Evans said calmly.

Suddenly he saw Alex and Charlie standing there.

"Hey, are you two okay?" he remarked, noticing their disheveled appearance. "I was worried about you two. Glad you're back. You almost missed all the fun."

"Mr. Evans – " Alex interjected.

"Follow me," the counselor directed and the two of them followed him to the other side of the bus.

There at the edge of the road Alex and Charlie could see trailers, camera equipment and people they didn't know.

"What's happening?" Alex asked.

"They're filming a movie!" Mr. Evans exclaimed. "Isn't that awesome? The crew has been setting up all around this ravine and our bus happened to break down right in this area. We've been watching a crew of make-up artists working on a bunch of actors. How cool is that?"

"Oh that's way cool," Alex murmured looking sideways at Charlie.

A bus turned off the road and parked in front of the broken down bus.

"Oh sorry, everyone. It looks like the show's over. Everybody get on the new bus. We're off to camp."

Mr. Evans began ushering everyone to the bus and checking his list to make sure no one got left behind.

Leeanna and Andrew were laughing as they boarded the bus.

"What were you two on about?" Andrew asked Alex and Charlie.

"You guys looked freaked out," Leeanna commented.

"Ah we were just messing with ya," Charlie joked.

"Alex?" Leeanna questioned.

"Yeah, that was just me and Charlie cooking up some pre-camp fun," Alex confirmed.

The engine roared to life and they were on their way to camp.

"So what happened to that potion challenged bird in that story we started before the bus broke down?" Andrew asked, changing the subject.

"The little kid jumped on the bird's back and together they traveled the world killing zombies by pecking them to death and ripping them apart," Charlie said finally.

"Oh, gross," Leeanna squirmed.

"Okay then," said Andrew.

"You couldn't ask for a better ending than that," Alex smiled at Charlie and looked out the window so she wouldn't explode with laughter.

CHAPTER TWELVE

After orientation, finishing dinner and tidying the dining hall everyone was invited to the big fire pit.

The assorted lawn chairs encircled the fire pit and after Mr. Evans gave basic instructions on how to light a fire in the wilderness, graham crackers, marshmallows and chocolate came out for a smores fest.

Andrew sat next to Alex and smiled at her as he kept passing her marshmallows. Leeanna sat on the other side of Andrew and demonstratively kept offering him more chocolate.

Charlie and Pete sat on the other side of the fire pit, trying to keep a lid on Jason's shenanigans.

"Who's up for a scary story?" Mr. Evans asked.

The kids murmured their approval with smore filled mouths. It was clear the kids already thought Mr. Evans was a pretty cool counselor.

Mr. Evans waited until he had everyone's attention. He slowly looked at everyone seated around the campfire and began in a low voice:

He sat in the old aluminum boat waiting for the fish to bite. He had put his good luck lure on, the same one he had caught his prize winning pike on during last summer's fishing derby.

He waited.

He waited.

He hoped his good luck hadn't worn off. He watched as the mist slowly cleared off the lake as the early morning sun filtered through the air. It was going to be a great day.

Aaron wasn't far from shore and he knew how to operate the fifteen horse powered motor on the back of the fishing boat. He had his red life jacket securely fastened around his ten year body, and was within hearing distance of his parents' trailer on the edge of the lake. He knew they wouldn't be angry with him for fishing even if it was six thirty in the morning.

He waited for the fish to bite.

He waited.

Then he felt a little tug at the end of his line. He gave the rod a quick jerk to be sure he buried the hook and began to reel in the line. The fish pulled back and Aaron cranked harder. He reeled the line in bit by bit imagining

130

the size of the fish according to the strength of its resistance. Aaron reeled harder. He grimaced as he continued to crank it in against the power of the fish. It had to be BIG. He knew it had to be even larger than the pike he caught last year. He pulled some more against the incredible power of the fish.

And then suddenly, the struggle stopped and the line fell slack, the lack of resistance tossing Aaron into the bottom of the boat. He didn't let go of the pole though. He managed to hang onto it.

He got up slowly, rubbing sore spots where he had hit the bottom of the boat and looked over the edge into the stillness of the water. The line hung limply.

Sadly, he began to reel in the line. It was easy now because the fish had obviously spit the lure.

He was turning the reel, thinking about the story he would tell his parents at breakfast about the big one that got away, when a gigantic reptilian head emerged from the muddy water and two menacing eyes looked directly at Aaron. Aaron stared back in horror as the creature's entire body began to emerge.

It looked like a monstrous, ancient turtle and it was at least three meters long and two meters wide with a heavily scarred shell protecting its body. Its eyes stared at him with a predatory glare and then it sank beneath the surface of the water.

Suddenly, the line went taut and the pole nearly escaped Aaron's hand. Quickly he grabbed it with both hands and held tightly as the creature tilted its huge shell and picked up speed.

Impulsively, Aaron tried to reel it in but as he started turning the handle he knew it was hopeless. There was no chance he could land such a prehistoric monster. So he hung on, just to see what would happen.

As the creature gained speed in the silence of the murky water, Aaron realized he could hear the soft rippling of water at the side of the boat. Peering over the edge he suddenly understood that the boat was moving at an astonishing speed. He was being dragged by the creature.

His muscles ached as he held on, completely forgetting that he was supposed to stay within view of the trailer. The creature swam faster and Aaron continued to hold on as the slight aluminum boat moved forward in the still water, the unknown creature acting as its new motor.

It pulled him across the lake, but still Aaron held on. It dragged him into a tiny channel and slithered through the bull rushes. And still Aaron held on.

The channel twisted this way and that like dozens of connected S's as the creature kept going.

Slowly, he realized he was being towed into a large lagoon encircled by towering pine trees which shielded the body of water from the outside world.

The creature's head popped out of the water and turned its slate gray eyes towards Aaron. He seemed to look surprised to see such a little boy holding on to such a powerful creature.

He kept on swimming until they reached the centre of the lagoon.

Then the creature just lay there like a submerged log with only his head floating above the water and looked at Aaron for what seemed like a long time. Aaron looked back and impulsively said, "What are you looking at?"

The creature turned his head from side to side as though it was thinking.

"I'm sorry you ate my hook," Aaron continued. "It must hurt. I can try to remove it if you want me to."

The turtle looked at him curiously.

133

They looked at each other for a long time as the silence of the lagoon encircled them.

The creature silently moved forward, its mouth hanging open, exposing the hook embedded in the side of its jaw.

Aaron reached for the tackle box, knowing he would find the pliers there because his father had taught him how to remove a hook.

Another turtle emerged.

Aaron rummaged through the tackle box as another turtle swam toward the boat. He searched in the bottom of the box but couldn't find the pliers.

The second creature came closer.

He found the pliers.

He reached over the edge of the boat to remove the hook from "his" turtle.

Two others appeared from behind a floating log. They looked at him menacingly and swam closer with effortless strokes.

Quickly and carefully he began removing the hook from the creature's mouth. He knew that it could have bitten his hand off at any time, and yet it waited patiently for him to remove the metal object.

134

As the others closed in Aaron worked more quickly, but more nervously. It was difficult working with wet tools under such pressure. What would happen when the other turtles reached the boat?

He grasped the hook with the pliers but he knew he would have to pull sharply in order to get it loose. He was worried he would inflict great pain on the creature.

Suddenly one of the other turtles rammed the side of the boat, knocking Aaron over, and simultaneously yanking the hook out of the creature's mouth.

BANG!!

Another creature rammed him from behind.

They had surrounded him now and it was clear they had decided they would be glad to have him for breakfast.

The turtle he had helped looked up at him with bright eyes as the others gathered together to line up for the kill. The creature's message was clear: GET OUT OF HERE.

Aaron picked himself up off the bottom of the boat and clumsily reached for the pull chord of the motor. He pulled.

Nothing happened.

The creatures were nudging the sides of the boat in an effort to knock him out of it.

He pulled the chord again.

Nothing.

The creatures continued to bat the boat around.

Aaron pulled the chord again, the motor coughed and started. It was the sweetest sound he had ever heard. He threw it in gear and sped away as fast as the motor would propel him.

Only once did he look back to see the creatures disappear beneath the surface of the water. The turtle he had helped, alone, remained above the water and watched as Aaron headed for the channel. Aaron was certain he saw that turtle smile.

CHAPTER THIRTEEN

"Jason's missing!" Leeanna blurted as she headed towards Alex. "Mr. Evans has been looking for you."

Alex was just finishing her breakfast in the dining hall.

"What?" she returned, alarmed.

"Leeanna," Mr. Evans calmly said as he approached the table. "Let's not get Alexandria upset. We're checking the washrooms, the cabins, the classrooms and the surrounding area. We'll find him very shortly, I'm sure."

Alex regarded him with wide eyed alarm. He doesn't know Jason, she thought.

Charlie and Andrew, sitting opposite her, rose from their seats immediately.

"I'm checking the woods. Maybe he's looking for zombies," Andrew joked.

"I'm going down to the lake," Charlie announced.

"I'm coming with," Leeanna proclaimed and followed Andrew.

"Come with me," Charlie turned to Alex who seemed incapable of making any decision at the moment.

Charlie turned and left the dining hall, Alex following speechlessly in his wake.

It wasn't long before they were at the shore line and Charlie scanned the edge of the lake with intense concentration.

"Wow," Alex caught up to him. "You're fast."

"I started jogging a couple of weeks ago," he said quietly as he checked the dock area.

"Really?"

"Yeah, it's kind of cool actually. It's very solitary. I like my peace and quiet."

"If you ever wanted a running buddy, I'll go with you."

"Cool," Charlie murmured.

Alex quickly scanned the lake.

"Oh God, where is Jason? What the hell was he thinking?" she blurted.

Charlie stopped in front of an empty space at the dock.

"That's a very good question Alex. What was he thinking? If we knew that we could find him faster."

The water rippled against the wooden dock.

"There's a boat missing," Charlie remarked.

138

Alex regarded the empty spot questioningly.

"You think so?" she asked.

"I'm pretty sure every slip was full yesterday when they gave us the camp tour."

"Do you think Jason could have taken a boat and gone out on the lake?"

"It's possible," Charlie reflected. "The good news is that all the boats have life jackets in them."

"That's assuming the little idiot put it on."

"Alex," Charlie said softly. "I'm trying to make you feel better. Work with me here."

"Sorry," Alex murmured. "What do you think we should do?"

"Hey Charlie, Alex," Andrew yelled as he and Leeanna approached. "No one's found Jason yet and Mr. Evans wants everybody back at the dining hall."

Alex and Charlie looked at one another but didn't move.

"Come on guys," Leeanna said encouragingly. "Let's go."

Charlie reached into one of the boats, grabbed a life jacket and began putting it on.

"We'll apologize later," Charlie muttered. "I think I know where he is."

He lowered himself into the boat and looked up at Alex.

Without hesitation she jumped into the boat with him and began securing a life jacket around her mid section.

"What in the world are you guys doing?" Leeanna exclaimed.

"Guys, this is not a good idea," Andrew advised.

Charlie pushed off with one of the paddles and worked on bringing the motor to life.

"Sorry guys," Charlie said. "Sometimes you gotta do what you gotta do."

They left a stunned Leeanna and Andrew behind as they headed out into the lake.

"Do you really think you know where he is?" Alex asked incredulously.

"Remember last night when Mr. Evans told that story about the turtles? Well Jason was talking about those turtles non-stop all the way to the cabin, before lights out, and the first thing out of his motor mouth this morning was turtles, turtles, turtles."

"Yeah, he's crazy about turtles, ever since he saw Finding Nemo when he was a little kid," Alex exclaimed. "So where exactly do you think he is?"

"I think he's trying to find that lagoon. He went on and on last night about how he thought Mr. Evans' story really happened and how the lagoon must really be near here. He was dying to know if those turtles really existed."

The motor propelled them around the lake to the other side. Alex and Charlie both instinctively surveyed the shoreline to make certain there was no sign of Jason.

Then they headed for the narrow channel that would take them out to the big lake. Last night Alex had briefly viewed the map of the area that hung on the big bulletin board in the dining hall. The big lake had many little channels running off it. Jason could be in any of these channels searching for those turtles. Alex swallowed nervously. This was not good.

"Charlie, could you say some more stuff to make me feel better?"

He smiled at her, a gentle, reassuring smile that made her feel inexplicably warm and comforted inside.

"We'll find him."

They entered a few little channels, looked around carefully, calling Jason's name as they went but there was no sign of him.

They tried a wider river that fed the lake and slowly made their way through the centre carefully looking right and left for any signs of the missing boat among the bull rushes, water lilies and riverbed vegetation that choked the river's edge.

And then they saw it.

The boat was over turned, its blue bottom glinting in the early morning sunlight. There was no sign of Jason.

"Oh God!" Alex gasped.

Charlie killed the motor, threw off his life jacket and dove under the abandoned boat. Before Alex even had time to react, Charlie's head appeared and he announced, "There's no one under there."

He grabbed the side of their boat and began hauling himself back into it. Alex did her best to help him get back in and they both sat in the bottom of the boat panting and shaking.

"And the good news is?" Alex whispered.

"He's not under the boat," Charlie exclaimed. "And I think the life jacket is missing so he must have put it on."

He grabbed his own life jacket and secured it over his soaking wet clothes.

"Okay, so he left the boat for some reason. Where would he go? Where could he go?" Alex wondered, as she reached forward and pulled a piece of vegetation out of Charlie's hair, chucking it over the side of the boat.

"Thanks," he murmured and looked thoughtfully at her with his bright blue eyes. "Where could he go?" he repeated.

He pulled the chord and the motor roared to life again.

"There's a lot of vegetation here," he remarked. "Let's get around this bend and see what's on the other side of these bull rushes."

"Good idea," Alex agreed.

As their boat brought them around they could see a beautiful, sandy, secluded beach along a stretch of the river's edge. Lying on the warm sand, tiny, gentle waves lapping at shoe covered feet, lay a body.

It was Jason.

CHAPTER FOURTEEN

Charlie shut the motor off as he beached them and they scrambled out of the boat.

Jason's head popped up.

"Hey dudes!" he exclaimed.

Alex gasped, her hands to her mouth. "You're okay," she screeched and threw her arms around her little brother.

"Yeah, I'm fine," he muttered looking somewhat embarrassed.

"What happened?" Charlie asked calmly.

"Well I kinda tipped the boat over and then I couldn't get myself back in. So I decided to hang out on the beach till I could figure out what to do."

"What are you doing here in the first place?" Charlie asked.

Jason looked sheepishly at Alex. "I wanted to find those turtles in Mr. Evans' story."

Alex's face was red with rage. "Are you insane? Do you have any idea how worried everyone's been? They're turning the whole camp upside down looking for you.

Charlie and I are going to be in so much trouble coming out here without permission to find you."

Jason was shaking a little and Charlie could see his eyes were starting to fill with tears.

"Sorry guys," he said with a quivering voice.

"Let's just get in the boat," Charlie suggested. "We'll deal with whatever consequences we get when we get back to camp."

Alex did not look like she was going to let it go that easily. Jason clamored into the boat and as she turned to say something to her brother, Charlie put a comforting hand on her shoulder. She turned to him and looked up into his calm, reassuring eyes.

"Let's let it go for now. I think he's learned his lesson," he whispered.

"Okay," she acquiesced.

As she sat next to Jason on the seat, he impulsively grabbed her hand. "Sorry Alex," he said softly. She patted his hand reassuringly as Charlie started the motor again and they drew away from the beach and out into the main channel.

After a few minutes of listening to nothing but the motor Charlie grinned and said, "Well, sport, any luck finding those turtles?"

Alex shot him a look that could kill but Charlie couldn't help himself.

"Really Alex, we've come all this way. We might as well find out for sure."

Charlie gave her another one of those "work with me" looks, so she let him continue.

"I think I saw a huge turtle shell in the water just before I tipped the boat," Jason exclaimed. "But then I guess I lost it and I kinda got freaked at the idea that there really were a bunch of gigantic turtles in the water with me. So I headed for the beach."

Alex noticed that Jason looked a little embarrassed in front of Charlie. It was the first time she realized Jason looked up to Charlie. Actually, given everything they've been through the last little while, Charlie is pretty amazing she thought.

"What's that over there?" Charlie asked suddenly, pointing to something in the water.

Jason jumped up.

146

Alex grabbed him and wrestled him back to his seat. "Okay, so now we know how you tipped the first boat you were in today," she said sarcastically. "Sit your butt back down, and stay down. It's a miracle you're still alive."

Jason gave her an uncharacteristically dutiful look and stayed seated.

"Where?" he asked Charlie.

"Over there," Charlie pointed to a spot by the bull rushes and moved the boat a little closer, shutting off the motor, allowing them to drift quietly in.

And then they saw it.

Lying amongst the weeds was a flat, gray, triangular shaped object about the size of a little kid's plastic sandbox. It was encrusted with years of dirt, decay and moss, scratches and random engravings covering its surface. As they approached the partially submerged item, the dappled sunlight warming its surface, it looked remarkably like a huge turtle shell.

"Wow," Jason exclaimed with undisguised reverence. "It's a prehistoric – "

"Boat cover," Charlie announced, as he lifted the edge of the old tarp with one of the boat's wooden paddles.

Jason's face fell.

147

"Do you think this old tarp is what you saw earlier? Could this be your turtle shell?" Charlie asked carefully, considerate of the younger boy's gigantic disappointment.

"Yeah, I guess so," Jason agreed. "Man this really sucks. I thought I made a great discovery."

"Sorry Indiana Jones," Alex joked wrapping a friendly arm around her brother's shoulder.

"Do you mind if we leave the Turtle Temple of Doom now and get back to civilization and the punishment that awaits us?"

"Okay," Jason hung his head with disappointment.

"Let's get outta here," Charlie smiled and pulled the motor cord.

Only this time the motor did not come to life.

CHAPTER FIFTEEN

The birds chirped animatedly, the leaves rustled in the trees at the water's edge as the three of them regarded each other with worried stares.

"Yup, we're outta gas," Charlie confirmed as he checked the boat's gas tank.

"What are we gonna do?" Jason wailed.

"Shh Jason," Alex exclaimed. "Charlie will think of something."

Charlie looked at her with an amazed expression on his face.

"He always does," she added proudly, smiling.

"Ooh, no pressure," Charlie quipped.

"Do you have your cell phone on you?" she asked, seizing on the idea that they could just call for help.

"Sure do."

He pulled his soggy phone out of the pocket of his still wet board shorts.

"Oops," he murmured as he wiped the excess moisture off.

"Do you think it'll still work?" Alex wondered.

"Maybe," Charlie checked for a signal. "Nothing right now. Welcome to Plan B," he announced as he grabbed the two paddles from the bottom of the boat.

He put them in the water and began awkwardly pushing and pulling to make them work.

Alex smiled. "Charlie, they're paddles not oars."

"What's the difference?" Jason put in.

"Oars can be operated by one person because they sit in special holders on the boat edge. The rule about paddles is that it's one per person. Here Charlie," she said and took one of the paddles from him. "You paddle on the right side, and I'll put mine in on the left side of the boat."

She turned around so they were both facing the bow, Charlie in the rear, Jason in the middle and Alex up front.

"Okay, start paddling," she instructed.

They paddled for a long, long time with the goal of following the river to the big lake. Hopefully there they would encounter other boaters who could help them.

"Hey Jason, buddy, you don't look busy. Could you grill a couple of burgers up for me and Alex?" Charlie joked.

"Onion rings on the side for me," Alex joined in, her muscles beginning to hurt.

"Why don't you guys let me take a turn?" Jason suggested. "I'm almost twelve you know, I'm not a baby."

Charlie nodded and Alex carefully switched places with Jason passing him the paddle.

"You get a break next," Alex announced to Charlie.

"No worries," he added.

They paddled some more as the sun rose higher in the sky.

"Look guys," Jason exclaimed excitedly awhile later. "I can see the big lake."

Charlie pulled out his phone again as Alex and Jason continued to paddle.

"I think it's done," Charlie proclaimed.

"It's totally my fault it ended up in the water," Jason admitted. "I'll use my allowance and get you a new one."

Charlie smiled at him. "You know for a goofball, you're a pretty decent kid. We'll talk about it later. Maybe I can still fix it when we get back to camp."

With a few extra strokes they emerged into the big lake. The waves were choppy and it was windy compared

151

to the protection of the river and the secluded beach. It would be hard to use the paddles here.

It wasn't long before Alex spotted a speedboat pulling a water skier behind it. The universal signal for distress was to wave your arms above your head, back and forth, left and right so Alex did just that.

Moments later the passenger in the boat, who was supposed to be keeping an eye on the safety of the skier, spotted Alex and motioned to the driver that they should go check things out.

"Awesome!" Alex squealed with delight. "That wasn't nearly as hard as I thought it would be."

After stopping to pull the skier into the boat, the speedboat headed their way. From a distance they were smiling and waving at Charlie, Alex and Jason. But something about the way the driver smiled at them, with a glassy eyed stare, gave Alex an uneasy feeling in the pit of her stomach. As they came closer she could see the driver and the passenger had beers in their hands. The skier was throwing a rope from boat to boat.

"Grab on," he directed as they came closer.

"Charlie, I have a bad feeling about this," Alex whispered.

Suddenly, behind the speedboat, Alex could see a police boat rapidly approaching them.

"Wow, Police," Jason announced, seeing the distinctive markings of the law on the water.

The guys on the speedboat hurriedly dumped their drinks in a cooler, pulled in the rope and sped away.

"Hey, you kids. We've been looking for you," the officer announced as they came up along side them.

CHAPTER SIXTEEN

Pete slipped the wriggling bull frog into the pocket of the pink jacket sitting by the pond. He carefully zipped up most of the pocket allowing a bit of space so the big guy could get air.

Everyone was milling around waiting to hear what consequences awaited Jason, Alex and Charlie for their morning adventures out on the big lake.

Lunch was just over and people were clearing the picnic tables when Alex and Charlie emerged from the main office.

Leeanna sprinted towards them and immediately began peppering them with questions.

"Whoa Leeanna," Andrew came up behind her. "Give them a chance."

"Thanks Andrew," Alex smiled gratefully. "We had to call our parents."

"Oh, yuck!" Leeanna groaned.

"And tell them what we did," Alex explained. "That was the worst part."

"I can imagine," Andrew commiserated.

"And we're on duty in the dining hall tonight and tomorrow morning," Charlie added.

"What does that mean exactly?" Leeanna questioned.

"We have to help the kitchen staff with meal preparation and clean up." said Charlie.

"Actually, I think we got off lucky," Alex put in. "Jason has to apologize to the whole camp for freaking everybody out and he has to share a few pertinent words to explain, especially to all the little kids, why what he did was wrong and dangerous."

"Oh brother," Leeanna murmured.

Alex was distracted by a bunch of little kids squealing by the water's edge. They were jumping around, flapping their arms animatedly and chattering excitedly.

Charlie started to head to the pond to see what all the commotion was all about.

Alex turned to go back to her cabin.

Andrew followed her.

"Where are you off to?" he asked good humouredly.

"I'm going to check on Jason. He's supposed to be writing out a carefully worded apology."

"Do you mind if I walk with you?"

"Of course not."

They headed towards the cabins.

"Hey Alex, I saw a big sign up on the bulletin board, you know in the dining hall," Andrew said awkwardly.

"Ah ha," Alex muttered.

"There's going to be a big dance tomorrow night for all the older campers. The little kids get a movie and then a scavenger hunt."

"Cool."

Andrew cleared his throat. "You're going to be there, right?"

"Sure, I don't see why not. Unless of course Mr. Evans thinks of more consequences to send my way. I thought I had him all figured out, but now I'm not so sure. He asked us, like seven times, if we'd seen anything in that lagoon."

"Anything?" Andrew wondered. "Like what?

Suddenly, there was a blood curdling, hair raising scream that sounded like it came right out of a horror movie.

Alex and Andrew turned simultaneously in the direction of the scream.

156

It was Leeanna.

CHAPTER SEVENTEEN

Leeanna was screaming and Charlie was howling with laughter as Leeanna's pink jacket slowly hopped over the sand and stopped at her feet.

Andrew, Alex and a crowd of campers had gathered around to see what all the commotion was about.

Leeanna looked at her sandaled feet, saw the enormous frog's head extending out of the partially zipped up pocket and squealed again.

"Who did this?" she gasped.

A little red haired boy wasted no time in ratting out the culprit by pointing directly at Pete.

"I saw him slip that frog in the jacket when it was sitting under that tree."

He pointed to the willow tree by the pond.

Leeanna directed a death glare at Pete and yelled, "Are you out of your mind? What were you thinking?"

"Which of those questions do you want me to answer first?" he said sheepishly.

With pursed lips, glaring eyes, clenched jaw, and hands rolled into fists at her side, Leeanna looked as though she was about to explode.

Pete helplessly tried to diffuse the Leeanna bomb by using pathetic attempts at humour.

"Well, it was just a little summer camp fun. You know mayhem and high jinks."

She just stared at him, incredulously speechless.

"I'm not always all business and goal oriented and performance driven, you know. I can be a fun guy," he justified weakly.

"A fungi," Leeanna repeated venomously. "You mean like a MUSHROOM!!"

"Not that kind of a fungi, I meant a fun guy," Pete joked nervously looking at his audience for support. "Get it?" He looked at Leeanna.

"Okay, that is kind of a funny little pun," Charlie put in as he bent down, opened the zipper and released the frog. The little red haired kid took the large bull frog and plopped it into the pond.

"Yeah, I get it!" Leeanna exploded. "You always act like you think I'm an idiot!"

"Ah, Leeanna – " Pete said softly. It was clear he was now trying to apologize.

She gave him one last death glare, turned and stormed out of the area. In a matter of seconds everyone went back to what they were doing before the frog incident and acted as though it had never happened. The frog enjoyed an early afternoon swim and seemed none the worse for wear after his exploration of the inside of the human girl's jacket pocket.

"Pete, are you okay?" Alex asked carefully.

"She hates me," Pete said dejectedly.

"What makes you think that?" Charlie joked, trying to cheer up his pal. "The death glare she gave you, or the fact that she called you a type of fungus?"

Pete looked genuinely stricken.

And then Alex understood.

"You like her don't you?" she asked gently.

He nodded his head up and down but said nothing.

Charlie looked surprised. "But you're always giving her a hard time. How's she supposed to figure out you actually like her?"

"You know what my IQ is? Never mind. Don't answer that. All my brain cells aren't helping me one bit in this department. I haven't a clue what I'm doing," he finished miserably.

"You have to be nice to her," Charlie advised. "Girls like it when you act like you care about them. About what they think and feel about stuff."

"Act like they care?" Alex remarked sarcastically. "Act, meaning they don't really care?"

Charlie rubbed his forehead nervously.

"I didn't mean act, like acting or pretending, I meant act as in showing they cared," Charlie began to get all twisted up trying to express himself. "Ah, hell, I'm no expert," he admitted defensively.

Alex smiled to herself.

"Okay, Pete, it looks like Charlie is saying you need to do something nice for Leeanna or say something nice to her. That might get her attention," she suggested.

"Oh, he already has her attention," Charlie chuckled.

"Putting a bull frog in her jacket pocket and watching it hop across a beach doesn't count," Alex remonstrated.

Pete started to walk away, his bright green eyes indicating he was obviously deep in thought.

"Where are you going?" Alex asked.

"To see if I can figure out how to fix this."

161

He left.

It was then that Alex noticed that Andrew was sitting at one of the picnic tables. He seemed to be waiting for her. She had forgotten that they had been on their way to check on Jason.

Charlie was watching the bull frog head out into the deeper areas of the pond as she quickly joined Andrew.

"Do you mind if I catch up to you later?" she asked. "I just have to talk to Charlie about something."

"Sure," he said somewhat reluctantly. "I'll see you later then," he said slowly as he got up from the table, regarding Charlie curiously as he left.

Alex joined Charlie as he sat quietly on the warm sandy area at the pond's edge.

Together they watched the frog enjoying the water, submerging and surfacing as though he were watching them. They watched insects skittering across the pond's surface, noticed the bull rushes bending in the breeze and listened to birds twittering in the trees. The quiet peacefulness of the place was intoxicating.

"Charlie," she said seriously without any preamble.

"Hmm," he murmured.

"A few times in the last few weeks it looked like you wanted to tell me something- something that was bothering you."

He turned his face and looked at her intently.

"We're like best friends, all of us in the Monster Mob are. You know if there's anything I can do to help, you know I will."

She looked at him encouragingly.

"I know," he said softly. "I just don't know if there's anything anyone can do," he added hopelessly.

Alex considered this carefully. "You may be right. But maybe sharing whatever it is might make you feel better. Just knowing you're not alone might help."

He was silent for a moment as he watched the frog disappear into the deeper water for the last time.

"I just don't want you to think of me any differently," he said sadly.

Alex impulsively took his hand in hers and whispered soothingly, "Okay, you don't have to tell me."

"My parents are getting a divorce," he blurted.

Alex's jaw dropped.

"There it is. It's out. That's what's been eating at me."

"Oh Charlie, I'm so sorry," she whispered gently, feeling incredibly sad for him. "I wish there was something I could say or do that would make you feel better."

He looked at her appreciatively, grateful for all the wonderful things that made Alex, well, Alex.

In that moment he knew he wanted to kiss her.

She was smiling up at him, her eyes swimming with tears. He smiled down at her, slowly leaned towards her and…

"Alex, Alex," Leeanna yelled as she ran towards her friend.

Alex hastily wiped her eyes, let go of Charlie's hand and stood up.

Leeanna, totally oblivious to anything but herself, thrust a piece of paper in front of her best girlfriend.

"Oh hi, Charlie," she said dismissively.

"What's this?" Alex asked with exasperated politeness.

"It's a letter," she said smugly. "The writer says I'm smart and beautiful and amazing, and you absolutely have to look at the last line."

Alex and Charlie looked. It said, "Je t'adore."

Leeanna's face was aglow with pleasure.

164

"That's French!" she exclaimed.

"Yeah, we know what it is," Alex explained. "It means "I adore you." We all take French." She stated the obvious.

"Who do you think would write to me in French?" Leeanna asked triumphantly.

Charlie and Alex remained mute.

"Andrew, that's who," Leeanna giggled. "Come on you guys. We have to get to our afternoon activities."

Leeanna grabbed Alex by the arm and led her away excitedly chattering on about the letter as Charlie followed silently behind.

CHAPTER EIGHTEEN

Later that afternoon Alex decided that the best thing to help Charlie take the weight off his shoulders about his parents' divorce would be to have his first wind surfing lesson.

She asked one of the camp instructors to act as a life guard on the beach of the little lake adjacent to the camp so she could take a wind surfer out for a little while.

"Oh, I don't think so," Charlie said reluctantly.

"Come on. It'll be cool. I'll show you how," Alex coaxed.

"Naw, I don't think so."

"Hey, would I waste my valuable time if I didn't think you could do it?" she asked teasingly. "Come on. You won't be sorry."

"Well, if you say so." He shrugged his shoulders, resigning himself to the idea. "Okay, I'll give it a shot."

He put on his mandatory life jacket. She put one on as well and they waded out into the lake, Alex dragging the surfer behind her.

"Wow, the water's cold," Charlie observed as they stopped in water that was about a meter deep.

166

"Wuss," Alex joked.

Charlie scowled at her and then smiled.

"All right," Alex began. "It's not very difficult but you do have to know a little trick. Now, this rope here attached to the mast, is the one you pull up on. You have to pull hand over hand like this," she explained, showing him the one potato, two potato motion. "And when you get to the top of the rope you should be right by the wishbone which gives you control over the sail. It's very important that you cross your left hand over your right hand to grab the wishbone. If you let go of the rope to grab the wishbone, you'll lose your balance every time. Trust me."

"I do," Charlie said simply.

For a moment their eyes met and they looked at each other as though they were both trying to figure out what the other one was thinking.

Alex broke the silence.

"Come on, up ya go."

Charlie got up on the board suddenly feeling very awkward and shaky as the water swayed the board beneath him. But somehow none of that mattered because Alex had looked at him in a way she hadn't before. Maybe he had a chance.

167

The board floated out a little further.

"Hand over hand Charlie," Alex called suddenly. "Get that sail up."

He grabbed the rope and began the hand over hand motion, slowly raising the water-filled sail out of the lake. As the sail rose, the air currents began to play with it and he started to feel the board turn beneath him.

"Faster Charlie," Alex yelled from the shallows. "Get the sail up and put your hands on the wishbone so you can steer."

"What?" Charlie yelled back.

"Hands on the wishbone!" Alex gestured frantically with her hands.

But the wind had grabbed the sail before he had had the chance to grab the wishbone and the sail plummeted back into the water.

Alex saw what happened and called out encouragingly, "Start again Charlie."

Determinedly, he began the hand over hand motion again and quickly crossed his left hand over his right to grasp the wishbone. Then he had it and the wind began to slowly push him ahead.

"Watch the ducks?" she hollered as she spied a group of ducks sitting in the bay for which Charlie was heading.

"What?" Charlie returned, not understanding her at all.

"The ducks!" she called again making ridiculous flapping movements with her arms.

And suddenly an explosion of quacks, a violent flapping of disgruntled wings and a quick skittering of feathery bodies across the surface of the water threw Charlie off balance. He plunged into the water as the mast fell behind him.

He emerged out of the water shaking his dark, wavy hair in disbelief.

"Well, it's not as easy as it looks," he quipped loudly.

"So you're saying you're not ready to audition for a part in Hawaii Five-O," she joked from a distance.

"So-o-o funny!" Charlie grinned.

He pulled himself back on the board, regained his balance and started the hand over hand motion again. This time he had more success and made it further out into the lake out of Alex's hearing range.

169

She watched as he rode the wind.

Charlie had never felt like this before. Suddenly he felt completely free, as though all that mattered was the sail board and how far the wind could take him. He hung on and slowly let the wind's power support his body. The water made little rivulets behind him, and struck the front of the board dividing itself and trailing off to the side.

After awhile Charlie reluctantly made his way back to the shore. He let the rope go and jumped off the board into the shallow water.

Alex was waiting there, smiling.

"Where did you learn how to do that?" Charlie wondered breathlessly.

"My aunt taught me at her cottage last summer."

"It's amazing," Charlie exclaimed. "It's like any problems you have just disappear into the wind."

"Exactly."

"It was totally awesome. Thank you, thank you, thank you!"

Charlie held on to the board with one hand and embraced Alex with his other arm.

"Hey guys," the instructor called from the life guard tower. "It's time to put that wind surfer away and get to the dining hall. Aren't you two on duty tonight?"

Charlie reluctantly released Alex and they both murmured, "Yeah."

They headed for their cabins to get changed and went to the dining hall to start phase one of their consequences.

CHAPTER NINETEEN

After peeling and cutting up potatoes and carrots, Alex and Charlie were asked to go make themselves presentable for dinner. It took several hand washings to get the orange carrot stains off their hands but all in all it wasn't so bad. They would still be allowed to go to the dance later tonight so a little kitchen duty wasn't the end of the world. Adults thought they were so smart. They had no idea that taking the dance away would have been far more painful than having to prepare some vegetables and later do some dishes.

"You're doing a great job," Mr. Evans smiled as Charlie and Alex stood behind the counter and served the steamed carrots and mashed potatoes to all the other campers and staff.

"Thanks," they said in unison.

Mr. Evans took his plate of food to the nearest table, set in down and went to the front of the dining hall.

Observing that most of the campers were sitting and eating, he raised his hand and addressed the crowd.

"All right everyone, listen up," he began in a pleasant but authoritative voice. "Jason has a few words he would like to say to us."

He motioned encouragingly and Jason came to the front of the room.

Alex watched from behind the counter. Charlie gave her a sideways glance of concern as he spooned some food on his plate.

Alex had to admit, Jason had some skill in the butt kissing department. He smiled at his audience, expressed his deepest concerns for worrying the camp during his little "mission" and assured everyone quite sincerely that such a thing would never happen again.

Yeah, right! Alex grinned to herself.

The audience applauded as though a show had just ended.

"Are you okay?" Charlie whispered.

"Yeah," Alex shook her head. "That kid's either going to be a brilliant actor or a top selling salesman when he grows up."

They took their plates of food and joined their friends at their table.

Alex sat opposite Leeanna who sat next to Andrew, so it would have been impossible for Alex to miss the way Leeanna flirted with him. She was a non-stop warm smiling, eyes glittering, hair flipping, infatuated teenage girl. It exhausted Alex just to look at her. Should it be that much work to attract a guy? Alex didn't think so.

Pete sat at the end of the table looking like he'd rather be any place but here. Andrew, totally oblivious to Leeanna, was talking to Pete about how he had been canoeing this afternoon and how tomorrow he was going to go rock climbing.

"Hey buddy, did you want to come along?" Andrew asked.

"Me?" Pete retorted. "Thanks man, but I don't know the first thing about rock climbing."

It must have nearly killed him to admit that he had limitations.

"I'll go with," Leeanna interjected.

Everyone swiveled their surprised heads in Leeanna's direction.

Andrew regarded her with fascination. "Wow I didn't think you of all people would be up for that."

She turned a frozen, speechless smile on him.

"I'm going to go get ready for the dance," she said suddenly and stood up from the table.

"See you there," she said to Andrew, waved to the rest of us and left.

Andrew said his goodbyes and slowly the other kids left the eating area, the teenagers getting ready for the dance and the younger kids looking forward to the movie and scavenger hunt.

Only Charlie, Alex and Pete were left silently shoving what was left of their food around and around their mostly empty plates.

"Oh, Charlie," Pete suddenly came back to reality. "Here's your cell man. I fixed it."

Charlie happily took his cell phone from Pete, giving him the fist against fist knuckles move as a sign of appreciative friendship.

"Thanks, man. Well, I'm off," Charlie announced. "I have to go and partake of all my beauty secrets before my grand appearance at this evening's events."

Alex laughed unabashedly, but it was clear as Charlie regarded Pete, that he had intended to throw some humour into the mix to cheer up a very dejected Pete. Charlie hopelessly shrugged his shoulders. Alex mouthed,

"I'll talk to him," as Charlie turned and left to help with the kitchen clean up.

"So Pete, what's up?"

Even though the room was empty except for the two of them and Charlie and the kitchen staff clinking dishes and cutlery, Pete leaned forward and whispered to Alex.

"I did what you guys said," he explained. "I did something nice for Leeanna."

He leaned back in his chair looking like he had just given his last pint of blood and there was nothing left to give.

"What did you do?" Alex tried not to sound as though the whole thing was going to turn out to be a disaster.

"I wrote her a little letter."

"What? What did you write?"

"I told her she was beautiful and amazing and that I adored her."

Alex swallowed as all the pieces suddenly fell into place.

"Pete," she leaned forward gently. "Did you tell her you adored her in French by any chance?"

"Yeah. Wow! I know you're an awesome mystery writer Alex, but how do you know that?"

"I'm no great detective Pete. She showed me the letter."

"Really. Oh!" He didn't seem to know what to say next.

"Pete, she thinks Andrew wrote the letter."

"What?" he blurted. "Oh, God."

"Well, in her defense, you haven't exactly ever acted like you liked her and Andrew was in French immersion for years, so she must have thought the French part was like a clue to the secret identity of the letter writer."

"Oh, God," he said again, more hopelessly this time.

"Just relax Pete," Alex said soothingly. "You go and get ready for the dance. I have to go help Charlie in the kitchen. We'll think of something."

"Thanks Alex," Pete said in a low voice.

"Hey, no worries. Andrew isn't the right guy for her anyway. I mean really, can you imagine Leeanna rock climbing?"

Pete chuckled in spite of himself. "Yeah, I'm having a hard time picturing that."

"Imagine what would happen if she ran into a frog part way up that wall," she quipped.

And then they both started howling with laughter.

By the time Alex made it to the kitchen Charlie was already gone.

"He finished his half," the cook gently informed Alex. "The rest is yours, sweetie."

The camp cook reminded Alex of her grandmother who had kind eyes, a warm smile and a soft tone of voice.

Alex got to work on the pots and pans, her smile never diminishing as she pictured Leeanna on that rock wall and wondered what exactly Charlie's beauty secrets were.

CHAPTER TWENTY

"Look at that spinning disco ball thing," Leeanna's pink painted finger nail directed Alex to the ceiling of the dining hall. "That's so retro I think it's actually cool."

A new song came on.

"I have to talk to you about something." Alex had decided that the only way to sort this mess all out was to tell Leeanna who actually wrote the letter so she could stop trying to impress Andrew, realize that they had virtually nothing in common, and maybe even give Pete a chance if she actually knew he had written the letter. She had tried all evening to get Leeanna alone long enough to speak privately.

"Oh, look, here come the guys," Leeanna observed, as Andrew and Charlie approached. "Don't they look awesome?"

Despite her need to talk to Leeanna, Alex turned and watched the boys approach. Andrew wore deep orange Hurley board shorts, a slightly softer shade of orange t-shirt and his short blond hair in a spiky, sporty-doo. Charlie's blue eyes sparkled to compliment his rich blue new age Batman t-shirt and charcoal gray board shorts.

"Hi ladies," Andrew said smoothly.

"Hi," Leeanna smiled, looking only at Andrew.

"Did we already mention you ladies are looking lovely tonight?" Andrew continued to pour on the charm, much to Leeanna's satisfaction. The girls were both wearing black capris and sandals. Leeanna wore a soft yellow Aeropostale t-shirt and after today Alex could not resist wearing her bright green Kermit the Frog t-shirt.

Charlie grinned. "Nice t-shirt," he said to Alex.

She tried not to burst out laughing.

"The running is agreeing with you," she said to Charlie. "You're looking awesome."

Charlie smiled a little self-consciously. "Thanks, Alex."

"I guess that must be one of your beauty secrets," she joked.

He laughed.

Pete, wearing a deep gray Darth Vader t-shirt and black shorts, joined the group.

"Hey guys, cool dance huh?" he said, hoping to find out what was going on between the four of them.

Alex seethed. Was she ever going to get to talk to Leeanna about Pete's letter?

180

"You know Pete, you kind of look like a vampire surfer dude with your blackish ensemble," Charlie joked.

Leeanna suddenly turned and looked at Pete. Surprised by the sudden attention, Pete's luminous green eyes stared at her as though he was a deer caught in the headlights of an oncoming car.

She stared back.

"Wow, Pete. I never really noticed how green your eyes are," she said simply.

He blinked.

"Come on Alex, let's dance," Andrew grabbed Alex's hand and headed for the area underneath the disco ball.

Leeanna stared, speechless, after them.

In a totally insane moment of reckless courage Pete stammered, "Hey Leeanna, wanna dance?"

She slowly turned her gaze from Alex and Andrew, not liking how Andrew embraced Alex with his arms around her waist during the slow dance.

Pete looked at her hopefully and then gallantly extended his hand to escort her to the dance floor in an old fashioned gentlemanly manner.

She blinked again and looked at him as though she had never really seen him before. As though they had not been friends, or friendly enemies aggravating each other and getting on each other's nerves for years.

"Your eyes remind me of the vampire in my story," she uttered without thinking.

He took her hand and wordlessly they began swaying back and forth to the soft music as though it was the easiest, most natural thing they had ever done. It was like they were in an enchanted movie like Beauty and the Beast.

And then over his shoulder she saw it.

The kiss.

One moment Alex seemed to be trying to say something to Andrew and the next second Andrew had leaned in and kissed her right on the mouth.

The spell was broken.

Leeanna pulled herself out of Pete's embrace and took a few furiously determined footsteps towards Alex and Andrew.

"How could you?" Leeanna cried at Alex and then ran out of the room.

Alex was speechless and flustered as she hastily scanned the dancing area. This looked bad: really, really bad.

Where was Charlie and how much had he seen and heard?

CHAPTER TWENTY ONE

Like a lone tree in an empty forest, Pete stood by helplessly in the wake of Leeanna's sudden departure.

"Go after her!" Alex directed him. "She's really upset."

Pete exited the dining hall in a flash. For a nerdy, techie guy he sure could run.

Alex turned to Andrew as others continued to dance around them, oblivious to their little drama.

"Andrew, what the hell were you thinking?" Alex exploded with quiet frustration.

"What are you talking about?" Andrew's face was a portrait of confusion. "You were going on about how Leeanna has this big crush on me, and how she's all wrong for me so I better let her down gently, and how I should look for some other more compatible girl."

"Yeah! So!" Alex said exasperatedly.

"So I thought you were talking about you."

"Me!" Alex exclaimed.

"I've always thought you were the coolest Alex, and kinda secretly, or not so secretly hoped I had a chance with you. I thought you were finally saying you liked me. I figured you wanted me to kiss you."

"Oh God, no."

He looked hugely embarrassed.

"I'm sorry Andrew. I didn't mean that to come out like that, it's just that with Leeanna liking you so much it wouldn't have been right to display something like that right in front of her. I would have had more respect for her feelings than that. And if I did really like you, you know, like that, I would have waited until Leeanna liked someone else so it wouldn't have hurt her if you and me got together."

"Wow, you have more integrity than anyone else I know."

"Hey, I have to live with myself. I have to own all my screw ups. We all do."

"I'm sorry, if I made you uncomfortable," Andrew apologized.

"Hey, me too. I'm sorry I erupted like that. We've all been best friends forever. I should have stayed chilled…" Alex's voice trailed off as though she had more to say but couldn't bring herself to put it together.

"What?" Andrew wondered.

185

"I'm pretty sure Charlie saw the whole thing," she whispered sadly.

Suddenly he saw what was actually happening here. Andrew smiled knowingly.

"Does he know how you feel about him?"

"What? No, maybe, I don't know. He's got a lot on his plate lately."

"The dance is shutting down," Andrew remarked as the main lights started to come on. "You should go find him." He was smiling the old familiar good friend smile again.

"Thanks, Andrew. You really are the coolest."

"Yeah, I am pretty cool aren't I?" he grinned in return.

Jason snuck in as Andrew left.

"Alex, Alex," he whispered excitedly, trying to stay invisible around the remaining stragglers.

"Jason, you're not supposed to be here."

"I know that. You have to come with me," he said grabbing her by the arm. "You're never gonna believe what I found during the scavenger hunt."

He pulled her into the hall, past the classrooms and around a corner to an area of the main building she had never been to before.

"Jason, we're not supposed to be here and I really don't have time for this," she snapped as she thought about trying to find Charlie.

Jason stopped abruptly before a dark wooden door with a tarnished brass name plate screwed to the surface. Alex just had time to notice the name plate said A. Evans, before Jason had pulled them both into the room and quickly shut the door behind them.

"Jason, what…?"

"Look!" he directed.

He pointed to a bulletin board behind an antique pine roll top desk. The cork on the wall was impaled with push pin after push pin holding up newspaper clippings exhibiting various stages of yellowing due to aging.

Alex's curiosity got the better of her and she ignored her little inner voice that was telling her she would have to own this mistake later. Like a magnet, she was attracted to the headlines of the newspaper articles. Her brown eyes grew wide and her jaw dropped in disbelief.

Jason grinned. "These articles, at least the headlines, I haven't had enough time to read them all, prove there have been turtle sightings in this area as far back as the 1870s."

He pointed to the dates under the by-lines of some of the articles. "This proves Mr. Evans' campfire story about the turtles is real."

Alex turned and looked at her younger brother with a mixture of terror and excitement.

"If I promise to help you take photos of all this stuff so we can examine it in peace and quiet without being caught for breaking and entering, can we please go now?"

"How are we going to get photos?" Jason wondered as Alex tried to drag him to the door.

"We'll use Charlie's cell phone," she whispered, hopefully.

"Okay," Jason said, and as he put his hand on the door knob an ear splitting alarm resounded throughout the building.

CHAPTER TWENTY TWO

Everyone who was left evacuated the main building and as Alex and Jason emerged as inconspicuously as they could, Alex began looking around for Charlie. People already in their cabins were emerging to see what all the commotion was about. Everyone was directed to stay in the beach area by the pond for safety and visibility while they waited for the fire department to arrive.

Jason and Alex regarded each other sheepishly hoping desperately that they had done nothing in Mr. Evans' private office to trigger the fire alarm.

In the gathering, talkative crowd Alex spotted Leeanna and Pete.

He had his arm looped through hers and he looked like he was trying to soothe and comfort her as he whispered into her ear.

Alex decided she would go and talk to them right now.

"Stay with your group and do what the counsellors tell you to," she directed Jason.

"I'll see you tomorrow," he said conspiratorially as he joined his friends.

"I need to talk to you guys now," Alex said determinedly as she directed Leeanna and Pete to slip over closer to the pond away from the crowd.

The fire department had arrived and entered the main building.

"Okay, look Leeanna, I'm so sorry about what happened at the dance. But it's not what you think, okay. I would never hurt you on purpose. I was trying to talk to Andrew about you, actually, trying to explain to him about how much you really like him and the next thing I knew he planted his lips on mine."

Alex deliberately left out the part where she was trying to coax Andrew into seeing that Leeanna was not the right girl for him because that might have been a mistake she would need to own later. She didn't want to hurt Leeanna with that now.

Strangely, Leeanna smiled at her.

"It's okay," she said giving her girlfriend an unexpected hug.

Alex looked at Pete for an explanation for Leeanna's perplexing response.

He said nothing and shrugged his shoulders.

Leeanna released Alex and said, "Pete has been with me the whole time since I ran out of the dance. We've been for a little walk and he's made me feel much better."

"Really?" Alex questioned giving Pete another "will you explain to me what is going on?" kind of stare.

"Pete was telling me he thinks Andrew's a really cool guy, but he's really not the right guy for me," Leeanna continued calmly. "He thinks Andrew can't actually appreciate my true beauty and intelligence and let's face it, even though Andrew is kinda hot, he is such a jock."

Alex rolled her eyes and looked at Pete.

"So you're going to get over this?" Alex confirmed hesitantly, looking back at Leeanna.

"Sure," Leeanna smiled with resignation. "Live and learn. What doesn't kill us makes us stronger right?"

"Right!" Alex said, hardly believing what she was hearing.

"Speaking of what could kill us," Leeanna continued. "Can you picture me rock climbing?"

Alex and Leeanna burst out laughing simultaneously and Pete tried hard to suppress a chuckle.

"So you're okay," Alex checked again.

"Absolutely," Leeanna said positively.

191

"Awesome," Alex smiled and turned to Pete. "Hey, buddy, we all know you're an absolute wizard with anything electronic, and you proved you can write an amazing mystery story, but I think it's time you let Leeanna know what an outstanding author of letters you are," she said pointedly.

As Alex left them she could see Leeanna's smiling, questioning face looking into Pete's surprised green eyes.

CHAPTER TWENTY THREE

As Alex circled behind the crowd she could see Mr. Evans in consultation with a fireman. Then he turned to the campers and explained that there had been a malfunction with the alarm due to a dust particle on a sensor or something and that everything was all right now. Everyone was instructed to go to their cabins. Alex fervently hoped that as all the campers dispersed she could slip unnoticed to the other side of the main building and head to the lake undisturbed.

Charlie was no where among the campers. She knew he must have wanted to be alone. He loved how free he felt on that lake when he was windsurfing. Maybe he was sitting quietly by the lake. She didn't know where else to look.

As she emerged beyond a small group of night covered trees, she spotted a lone figure sitting on the edge of the dock illuminated by the moonlight.

She approached quietly.

"Charlie."

He turned abruptly, his feet making a rippling noise in the water. Alex bent over, took off her sandals, sat down next to him and slid her feet into the water.

A loon called hauntingly in the distance and moonbeams danced off the surface of the lake.

"What a pile of fire works," Alex remarked.

"Yeah, I came down here to get away from the fire alarm craziness."

"Charlie, I'm not talking about the fire alarm," she took a deep breath and continued. "Did you see Andrew kiss me?"

Charlie turned his ankles in the water skimming his toes over the surface.

"Charlie?" she asked again.

"Yes," he blurted.

"I was talking to him about Leeanna since he kinda pulled me out onto the dance floor," Alex explained. "I had this crazy idea that I could get him to see that Leeanna was not the right girl for him, you know, so our buddy Pete had a chance, and the next thing I know …"

"He kissed you," Charlie said quietly, a great degree of emotion suppressed in those few words. "He likes you," he added dismally.

"Well, no, maybe, it's confusing. He might have thought he liked me at some point, but after I got through talking to him he's really clear I don't like him. Not as anything other than a great friend."

Charlie turned to her, his blue eyes sparkling in the moon light.

"So you don't like him?" he asked, trying to hide a spark of hope.

"No," Alex explained gently. "It was a huge misunderstanding. When I was babbling on about how Leeanna wasn't the right girl for him, he thought I was putting myself forward as the woman of his dreams."

Charlie smiled.

"You know what the worst part is though?" she continued.

"What?"

"I had this really cool romantic notion of what my first kiss would be like. There'd be a romantic setting and we'd be looking into each other's eyes and then we'd kiss and it would be amazing and magical. Instead I got this sloppy, cold, wet kiss from a guy who I'm not into at all."

"You sound seriously disappointed," Charlie remarked watching her carefully.

195

"I am."

"So you don't like Andrew?"

"Nope."

"Are you sure?"

"Double, triple, quadruple sure," she grinned. She looked down at her reflection in the water.

In silence he turned and looked out at the calm, glassy surface of the lake again. There were lights twinkling on the other side of the water. Charlie wondered if there were cabins over there. He didn't think the campgrounds extended that far.

"Do you like anyone else?" he asked abruptly.

"Yes," she whispered.

They turned and looked at each other very slowly.

"If you look between your feet at the surface of the water, you'll see the face of the guy I really, really like," she said shakily.

After the first surprised moment of understanding, he took her chin in his hand, smiled at her and kissed her. His mouth was soft and warm and velvety and delicious all at the same time. She wrapped her arms around his neck and drew him closer. He slipped his arms around her waist holding her gently, yet protectively at the same time.

Feeling suddenly overwhelmed their mouths parted and they hugged each other, their breathing ragged and irregular as though they had just been running.

"Wow," Alex murmured into his shoulder.

"Yeah, wow," Charlie admitted. She could feel he was shaking slightly.

"It was even better than I imagined it," she looked up at him.

He smiled, the most contented smile she had ever seen, and she put her head back on his shoulder.

They looked out at the lake again. Another loon called into the night.

"I guess we'd better get back to our cabins before we get caught," Charlie suggested sensibly.

Alex shook her head in agreement.

They walked hand in hand up the dock.

"Oh, Charlie," she said suddenly. "You're never going to believe this."

"Try me. I think tonight I could just about believe anything."

"You know Jason and that turtle story," she began.

"Ah man, he's like a dog with a bone about that thing."

197

"I know, I know," Alex admitted. "But I think he may have found something this time. I need to borrow your cell phone tomorrow so we can take pictures of some articles Jason found. He thinks he can prove those turtles really exist."

When Alex finished explaining what Jason had found and where, they stood in front of the girls cabins.

"We could get into so much trouble," Charlie warned.

"I know," Alex returned mischievously smiling up at him.

"And you think I'm going to help you with this turtle thing and do pretty much anything you want me to, just 'cause I'm crazy about you?"

"Pretty much," she chuckled quietly so no one would overhear them and then as she backed away she blew him a kiss, trying not to burst out laughing.

He grabbed her hand, pulled her close to him, and kissed her quickly before she could say anything else.

When he released her, he whispered, "Dang," grinned and turned to go to his cabin.

She whispered "Good night," and almost tripped up her cabin steps.

CHAPTER TWENTY FOUR

After Charlie and Alex finished their obligatory kitchen duty they activated the plan the Monster Mob had surreptitiously made at breakfast.

Charlie went with Jason, slipped into Mr. Evans' office, took photos of the newspaper headlines displayed on the camp counselor's bulletin board and sprinted to the boys' cabin.

Alex, Andrew, Pete, and Leeanna were already waiting nervously for their arrival.

They huddled around Pete's bed as he pulled his knapsack out of a dresser drawer. He gently slipped his laptop out of his backpack and placed it on the bed. He began pulling out cords, hooking Charlie's cell phone up to his computer and enlarging the photos.

"I asked the whole Monster Mob to get together because I think we might have a real life mystery here," Alex explained.

Jason grinned proudly.

"I guess you'll be one of us if you have brought a mystery that's worthy of our association," Pete explained with supreme authority and then grinned at Jason conspiratorially.

"Oh, I think I have," Jason assured them enthusiastically.

"Jason," Alex explained. "You should know that we started this group because we all felt like outsiders at our school. Do you know how we came up with the name Monster Mob?"

"No," said Jason.

"Oh boy, here she goes," Leeanna quipped. "She'll be happy to explain it to you."

Alex ignored her. "In 1816, a young Englishwoman named Mary Shelley and some of her friends were on vacation in Switzerland. It was raining and they were bored so they decided to write creepy stories to entertain one another. One night she had a terrible dream, woke up, and began writing Frankenstein. She was only nineteen years old at the time."

"Seriously?" Jason interrupted. "A nineteen year old wrote that?"

"The thing is," Alex continued, "Victor Frankenstein, the main character, was a medical student in Geneva and it was his secret wish to triumph over death so he performs these crazy experiments and ends up creating a creature out of dead body parts. Because the creature is not beautiful he rejects him and abandons him, and the poor creature spends the rest of his life trying to find love and acceptance. His pain turns to violence in the tragic ending. Everyone treated him like he was a monster but he was just an outcast. So we called ourselves the Monster Mob in honour of the excluded and unaccepted."

"And no one else could think of a better title than Alex could," Andrew joked.

"And it had a nice alliterative ring to it," Leeanna added.

"And here we have it," Pete announced.

Everyone crammed in to get a glimpse of Pete's computer screen with the enlarged photos.

"Look at this," Charlie pointed to the top of one of the articles. "This one's dated July 6, 1870."

The articles all described mysterious turtle creatures in various parts of the lakes, lagoons and channels in the vicinity but there were only hand drawn sketches. It seemed due to the haphazard appearances and unpredictable locations, no one had managed to take an actual photograph to date.

Quickly they scanned the articles observing many different dates up to the most recent, 2009.

"This article says the land our camp is on used to be owned by a Ms. Riley and that she sold a large portion of her land for the development of a camp for kids back in 1993," Andrew read.

"This reclusive guy, Mr. Hawthorn, wouldn't sell any of his land to make the camp," Alex added, pointing to another part of the same article. "Sounds like he just wanted to be left alone."

Suddenly, there was a knock on the door.

CHAPTER TWENTY FIVE

"Quick, get under the beds," Andrew whispered to the girls.

Alex and Leeanna dove under the beds. Pete tossed the sleeping bags over the edges to drape off the area beneath the beds, giving the girls more cover. Charlie opened the door slowly.

"Hey guys," Mr. Evans began.

Jason and Charlie looked at each other nervously. Had Mr. Evans discovered they'd been in his office? How would they explain their way out of this predicament?

"It's time to get to your morning activities," Mr. Evans continued. "This morning there's pond study, canoeing and archery. What are you still doing in your cabin?"

"We're on our way," Charlie smiled, trying to cover everyone's nervousness.

Mr. Evans smiled back and then looked past Charlie to the unmade beds.

Charlie, Pete, Andrew and Jason all froze as Mr. Evans seemed to be staring at the beds.

Agonizing moments went by as Mr. Evans seemed lost in thought and the boys were speechless with anxiety. Why wasn't he leaving?

"All right, at ease soldiers," he suddenly joked. "It's time to head out."

He turned to leave and as Charlie was beginning to close the cabin door, Mr. Evans stopped, turned and said, "Oh, guys, make those beds up before you go, would you?"

"Sure thing Mr. E," Charlie returned, and slowly closed the door.

"Don't," Pete whispered as he heard the girls begin to rustle beneath the beds. "Wait."

They all waited silently as Jason carefully peeked out the window to make sure Mr. Evans wasn't coming back.

"Coast is clear," Jason announced after several moments.

"Wow, that was close," Leeanna murmured as she dusted herself off.

"Too close," Alex added. "That would have looked really bad for all of us."

"Okay, you girls get outta here," Andrew suggested. "We'll meet you at the main hall in a few minutes. We better get to those morning activities or there'll be no staying out of trouble."

Leeanna noticed the warm and silent look Charlie and Alex exchanged as the girls left the cabin.

"So what's up?" Leeanna asked as the girls walked.

"What do you mean?" Alex returned.

Leeanna smiled at her. "You have kind of a happy glow about you this morning and you snuck into the cabin last night after everyone was already in bed. Were you by any chance with Charlie after the dance?" She certainly had a way of getting straight to the point.

Alex could feel the colour warm her face.

Leeanna laughed.

"We really like each other," Alex mused, as she thought about how she felt when Charlie had kissed her. "Oh, wow, that sounds really lame when I say it out loud."

"No it doesn't," Leeanna laughed as she put an affectionate arm around her friend's shoulder. "It's just because you've always been Adventure Alex, Mystery Alex and I'm immune to guys' charms Alex, that it's so funny. So you finally fell for one of them. Well, I'm proud of you honey. You're a big girl now," she giggled.

"Oooh, you're so funny, mocking me."

"Ah, Alex, it's just too much fun not to."

"Well, Lee, how long are you going to hold out on giving me the inside information on you and Pete," Alex returned fire.

Leeanna blushed instantly and Alex laughed as Leeanna shook her head back and forth as though there was nothing to say.

"Ha, it appears two can play this little game. And don't even start acting like nothing's going on, Lady Macbeth, because I already think "thou doest protest too much."

"Oh, so you're going to use Shakespeare against me," Leeanna said dismally.

"Yup."

They were almost at the main hall and Alex was afraid she was going to run out of time to get the story.

"Come on, spill it," she teased Leeanna.

Leeanna stopped, took her arm off Alex's shoulder and said very seriously, "Pete confessed that he wrote the letter. Of course I was stunned because I really thought Andrew wrote it. But after everything that happened last night, I do see that Andrew is not the right guy for me."

"Do you think Pete might be?"

"I never knew Pete thought so highly of me Alex. I mean the letter was sweet and beautiful and last night he was so kind and patient and attentive, and – " Leeanna grinned, "He does have those amazing green eyes like the vampire in my story."

"And he does look pretty good in black," Alex joked. "So there's a chance?"

"Life is full of chances," Leeanna returned enigmatically as they joined the boys at the main hall.

"I signed us up for the pond study," Pete said to Leeanna as she stood next to him. "I hope you don't mind."

"That sounds lovely," she smiled up at him. "Are you trying to help me overcome my fear of frogs?"

He smiled and squeezed her hand. "I thought I'd try. You'll probably enjoy them more in their natural setting than zipped into your jacket." He looked painfully apologetic.

Leeanna laughed unashamedly. "Good point."

She gave Alex a little wink as she and Pete headed off to the pond area.

Jason decided to go with Andrew to the archery targets and Charlie and Alex headed for the canoes.

Alex sat up front and Charlie paddled in the back. They dipped the paddles in the water and peacefully glided across the surface.

"Charlie, I was thinking," Alex began.

"Oh, oh," he joked.

She turned and grinned at him. "I think there might be a house back there," she pointed to the far side of the lake. "I thought I saw something when the Police brought us in. Do you think there might be someone living there, someone we could talk to about those turtle sightings?"

"Last night when we were sitting on the dock I thought I saw lights coming from over there. There might be a house there," Charlie agreed.

"Let's go," Alex exclaimed.

"Seriously? You wanna just canoe across the whole lake and show up on someone's door step and ask them if they've seen any prehistoric looking gigantic turtles?"

Alex shrugged her shoulders. "Do you have anything more exciting to do?"

"I could think of a couple of things," Charlie said softly as he leaned towards her. The canoe started to rock.

"Sit down Charlie, you'll tip us over," Alex laughed.

"Sorry," Charlie whispered and smiled sheepishly.

"Come on, it'll be fun."

Alex turned to the front of the canoe and began paddling again.

"I will follow you, Helen of Troy, though it be to my death," he said mockingly.

"Wow, overact much?" she joked as they continued to paddle.

It was breezy as they made their way across the lake and seagulls soared overhead checking out the breakfast buffet the lake offered. Alex felt like they were paddling against the current and it was hard work to keep going.

"Are you sure about this?" Charlie asked tentatively as they neared the other side.

"We're not doing any harm Charlie, we're just going to say hello and see if we can get any more information about whether these turtles really exist."

"Yeah, but that one article said that guy who hung on to his property was reclusive. That means he's not going to wanna see us."

"How do you know this place is his? That article was written awhile ago. How do we know he's even still here?" Alex countered.

209

They reached the other side and a newly constructed, freshly stained dock came into view.

Alex placed her paddle in the canoe and Charlie slowly steered them along side the dock from the rear. She jumped out and held on to the front as Charlie wordlessly got out and tied the vessel to a shiny metal ring secured to the dock.

They walked away from the water and headed up through the trees.

"I have a bad feeling about this," Charlie murmured more to himself than to Alex.

"Not afraid of zombies are you?" Alex joked.

"Hey, the way I remember it, you were just as freaked out as I was!"

Alex smiled and kept walking up the hill, carefully maneuvering over some rocky, moss covered areas. She stopped when she entered a clearing. Charlie was right behind her.

He slipped his hand into hers as they stood and stared at the beautiful old cabin surrounded by tall pine trees swaying in the strong wind. The structure was made of granite stone and huge hand hewn logs. It exuded the antique charm of a Christmas card minus the snow.

"Gee, d'ya think the Seven Dwarfs live there?" Charlie quipped.

And then the front door opened.

An elderly man stood in the doorway, tall and proud and enraged at the two teenage trespassers who stood before him. In three steps he was across the quaint wooden porch and heading down the steps towards them. Neither of them failed to miss the shot gun held by his left arm, and the enormous Rottweiler attached to the leather leash wrapped around his right hand.

Alex squeezed Charlie's hand so tightly he winced.

"Get off my land," the man growled at them as he, the dog and the shot gun came closer.

Neither of them moved, not because they were brave or defiant, but because they were both paralyzed with fear.

"This is private property," the man's anger brewed, and seemed to intensify as they stood still. "Get off my land and don't ever come back."

He stood only a few meters from them now. Up close his grey beard and long, unkept hair made him look as wild and unpredictable as a wolf.

211

Alex suddenly found her voice. "We're very sorry sir. We didn't mean any harm." She tried to sound confident even though she knew she was shaking.

"We'll leave now, sir," Charlie added in an attempt to calm Alex. "We're very sorry for disturbing you and your dog."

The large, extremely muscular dog made a low growl deep in its throat as the morning sunshine glinted off its ebony coat.

Both Alex and Charlie were instinctively afraid to turn their backs on the dog in order to leave and so they stood riveted to the spot.

Suddenly, the silver haired man and the dog turned and headed back to the cabin. Spontaneously, Charlie and Alex ran, slid down the embankment like a re-run of the zombie terror, sprinted urgently through the trees and skidded to a breathless halt at the dock.

The canoe was gone.

CHAPTER TWENTY SIX

They both froze, their eyes meeting in puzzled fear. Charlie bent down to feel the metal ring where the canoe rope should be as though he doubted his eyes telling him the boat was gone.

"I'm so sorry Alex," he whispered miserably. "I guess I really suck at tying knots. I was never a boy scout."

He stood up forlornly and Alex wrapped her arms around him.

"It's okay," she whispered into his shoulder. "We'll think of something."

"You're shaking," he observed, holding her protectively.

Suddenly she remembered how just this morning Leeanna had called her Adventure Alex and Mystery Alex and here she was practically crying into a guy's shoulder like the damsel in distress.

She gently pulled away from Charlie's warm embrace. "Okay, let's get a grip," she said determinedly. "We need to think, consider our surroundings, make due with what we have. I don't suppose you have your cell phone on you?"

"As a matter of fact I do," Charlie boasted and then regarded it ruefully. "No service."

"Of course," Alex grunted, looking across the lake. "How far do you think the camp is? I can see it from here."

"Too far to swim, if that's what you're thinking," he returned with undisguised alarm.

"Okay, Plan A: canoe, and Plan B: swim, both out of the question. We need a Plan C."

"Do ya think?"

"Okay, brainiac, you come up with something,"

They both looked around checking out the shore's edge and the underbrush of a group of trees hoping the mean old guy and his dog would not descend upon them while they were desperately trying to come up with an idea.

"Hey, look at this," Alex pointed to a pile of wood behind the clump of trees.

Charlie began pulling at one end of the old cedar.

"It's attached," he remarked. "I think it's an old dock. Look, a large section of boards are still attached like the old guy just chucked it here so he could put up his new dock."

They looked at each other. "Are you thinking what I'm thinking?" Alex remarked.

214

They both began hauling the wooden structure out from behind the trees and dragging it to the water. About ten boards were still joined together and sitting at the water's edge it looked remarkably like a raft. Charlie went back to the pile of wood, grabbed two loose boards and dropped them on top of the makeshift raft. He pushed it out into the water.

"Hey," Alex stopped him.

"Just a second. I'm going to see if it floats. There's no point in us both getting soaked."

He pushed off, grabbed a piece of board and began awkwardly paddling. He went out a few meters, the wooden platform holding him nicely, and turned around to collect Alex.

And that was when he saw the old man and the black dog standing on the crest of the hill looking menacingly down on them.

Charlie paddled urgently.

"Jump!" he yelled as he neared the shore.

Without question, Alex jumped onto the raft and the force of her body propelled them quickly away from the shore and into the current of the lake.

"Nice paddling," Alex remarked.

"Good thing you taught me so well."

They paddled steadily although awkwardly with the old dock boards as paddles. The current, working in their favour coming this way across the lake, helped them make it back to camp very quickly.

Without anyone paying attention, they hurriedly borrowed a little aluminum run about with a fifteen horse motor on the back of it to retrieve the lost canoe. It turned out to be conveniently beached in a little lagoon one property over from where it had drifted away.

Alex grabbed the rope at the front of the canoe and began attaching it to the little motor boat when a smiling lady, holding a steaming coffee mug in one hand and a book in the other emerged from the trees at the lake's edge and walked along her dock. A fluffy, grinning Shetland Sheepdog trotted by her side as she approached them encouragingly.

"Can I help you?" she asked pleasantly.

"I'm sorry Ma'am," Alex apologized. "We lost our canoe, so we just came to grab it."

"We didn't mean to trespass," Charlie explained as he quickly helped Alex tie the canoe to the boat and they were off.

216

"No problem," the lady called after them kindly, looking a little sad that they were leaving so suddenly.

"Wow," Charlie remarked as they bolted away. "That lady looked almost like she would have invited us for lunch, while the other guy looked like he would have liked to eat us for lunch."

Alex didn't laugh at Charlie's attempted humour. She was thinking.

They sped back to camp as fast as the little boat would take them with the canoe dragging behind, tied both boats up to the camp docks and breathed a sigh of relief.

"Charlie, did you get a good look at that lady? I was a little focused on tying up the boat."

"What about her?" Charlie wondered, as they headed to the dining hall for lunch.

"Don't you think she looks like the sweet elderly lady that sometimes helps in the camp kitchen?"

Charlie turned to say something when Pete and Jason approached them and began chattering non-stop about the morning's activities.

"Look, Jason and I did some more digging after we got back to the cabin. I Googled that Hawthorn guy," Pete

217

whispered, looking over his shoulder to see if anyone was within ear shot.

"It turns out Hawthorn's son died, when he was with the Canadian military back in '92. Maybe that's why he's kind of been a recluse ever since and didn't want any camp near him when it opened in 1993 because having kids around reminded him of his son and it was just too painful."

Charlie and Alex regarded each other skeptically. Could the bitter, angry man they met this morning be Mr. Hawthorn? And was the nasty man they met really just a guy enduring the burning pain of such a loss?

"The most turtle sightings are still on this guy's waterfront," Jason reminded them. "I think we have to go check this out," he said excitedly.

"Well, what do you think we should do?" Pete looked to Alex and Charlie.

"I think we should go eat lunch," Alex said practically. "I'm starving."

She started to head towards the dining hall door. The others followed.

CHAPTER TWENTY SEVEN

That evening as the campers sat around the fire telling stories and making smores, the Monster Mob carefully activated their latest plan to get more information to solve the mystery of Mr. Hawthorn and the turtles.

"So Mr. Evans," Leeanna began sweetly. "How many years have you been a camp counselor?"

He passed a bag of marshmallows to Jason and said, "Actually, my Mom and Dad bought this camp eighteen years ago. I spent every summer here since I was ten years old. A lot of good memories here," he added whimsically.

"Where are your parents now?" Pete asked.

"They're up at Algonquin Park on a camping trip. My Mom's a painter and she does landscapes up there every summer and they usually go for a weekend in the fall."

"Cool, kind of like the Group of Seven," Andrew said admiringly. "I recently saw their work at the McMichael Gallery. I have to admit, it's pretty awe inspiring."

Other kids shook their heads in agreement.

"My parents will be back next week," Mr. Evans added.

"So, what's the deal with the turtle story?" Alex dug in. "Are you the little kid in the story?"

Mr. Evans looked at the campers huddled around the fire. Their large fire reflecting eyes looked up at him expectantly, their marshmallows impaled on sticks hanging over the roasting flames.

"Well," he admitted reluctantly, "When I was ten, and I was out fishing, I did think I saw a gigantic turtle out in the lake. So that part is true. But the rest of the story with all the other turtles and the little kid and his boat getting dragged to a secret lagoon, that part has kind of been embellished over the years for dramatic effect."

Most of the kids groaned in disappointment, but some of the little kids looked quietly relieved to think that the turtles were just make-believe.

"So you really think you saw something though?" Alex pressed.

"Well, it was a long time ago Alex, I was only ten years old and memories fade or change with time, but yeah, I did think I saw something," Mr. Evans admitted.

"You know there have been turtle sightings in this area as far back as the 1870s," Jason informed them.

"How do you know that?" Mr. Evans wondered.

Jason froze. He would only know that if he'd been in the camp counselor's office.

"We Googled it," Pete came to his rescue. "So maybe you did see something when you were a little kid."

Jason breathed a sigh of relief.

"Well, my Dad thought my story was good for perpetuating the myth for camp publicity. He thought it would make people want to come to our camp if there was a chance they'd see the mysterious turtle. I'm pretty sure he thinks anyone claiming the story to be real is a bit of a goof ball, myself included," Mr. Evans chuckled.

"The old man who lives on the other side of the lake," Charlie pointed in the direction of the property with the old cabin, "Is that Mr. Hawthorn?"

"Yes," Mr. Evans said warily. "How do you know about him?"

"He came up in the Google search about the turtle myth in the area," Charlie explained.

221

"Don't go any where near that property," Mr. Evans advised. "That old guy is very territorial and doesn't want to be social. He likes to keep to himself."

The crackling of the fire and soft night sounds of the woods beyond slowly dimmed as people began to continue to eat and talk amongst themselves. Leeanna whispered to Alex, "Hey, who's that cute girl sitting next to Andrew?"

Alex regarded the tall willowy girl with the strawberry blonde hair. She was laughing and accepting a smore that Andrew had cooked for her.

"Oh, that's Erica. They met at archery," Alex explained. "She seems nice."

"Leeanna," Pete interjected. "I'm going to the kitchen to grab a drink. Can I get you something?"

"I'd love an ice tea," she smiled up at him.

"Coming right up," he smiled back warmly and as he turned to leave almost tripped over Jason's feet.

Jason leaned across Pete's empty chair and whispered to Alex and Leeanna, "We are so going to check out that turtle at old man Hawthorn's."

CHAPTER TWENTY EIGHT

Alex could hardly believe that it was already the fourth day of camp. So much had happened in such a short time. She didn't know which was more unbelievable: that she and Charlie had kissed, or that the Monster Mob was actually investigating a real life mystery.

After breakfast Charlie pulled Alex aside as she was on her way back to her cabin to get ready for pond studies.

They stood behind a large tree as others passed them.

"Alex," he said seriously. "I got a call from my Mother."

"Cool, your cell phone actually worked?" she joked.

He reached out and took her hand. "She's in town and she'd like to get together with me today, have lunch and stuff."

"Is everything okay?" Alex returned, concerned.

"She's fine. I think she just misses me, you know, considering all the stuff she must be going through with the divorce and all. I haven't even heard from my Dad, which is just as well because right now I'm so freaking mad at him, I'd probably say all the wrong stuff and make everything worse."

"Where's Ashley?"

"She's at a friend's cottage."

"Well then you should absolutely go see your Mom."

"You don't mind if I leave for a few hours?"

"Of course not," she said firmly. "I mean, I'll miss you," she smiled sweetly up at him. "But you're just leaving for a little while to help your Mom. You're a great son," she added admiringly.

"Thanks, but I really want you to think I'm a great boyfriend too, so I don't just want to leave you."

Alex was momentarily stunned. Boyfriend. He had called himself her boyfriend.

"You are a great boyfriend," she murmured as they slipped their arms around each other in a warm bear hug.

"Now go," she directed, pulling gently away. "I'll see you in a few hours."

She headed back to her cabin with a smile and a wave as Charlie headed to the main hall to get a ride into town with Mr. Evans. Apparently, he needed to buy more marshmallows for the next camp fire night.

They ate an early lunch that day after spending the morning busy with camp activities. Alex really had had no idea how many tiny creatures lived in a bucket of pond water until she survived the organisms' analysis of the pond studies course. It really gives you humbling insight into how many species are affected when humans pollute a waterway.

"Follow us," Leeanna and Pete said as they met up with Alex outside the dining hall.

Jason and Andrew joined them at the docks. Pete and Leeanna quietly slipped into a little fishing boat and secured their life jackets. Andrew and Jason slipped into a second boat and did the same.

"Get in with us," Andrew directed.

"What are we doing?" Alex asked suspiciously, eying Jason with skepticism.

"We're going for a little tour?" Leeanna grinned.

Alex stood on the dock, her arms folded resolutely. "Where to?"

"The other side of the lake," Pete explained. "We're going to see if we can solve a little mystery."

"Uh, uh. This is not a good plan. You weren't there when Charlie and I met up with Mr. Hawthorn. He had a gun and a vicious dog. Seriously guys, this is a bad idea."

"We're just going to pretend we're fishing," Andrew claimed, holding up a tackle box.

"That's our cover," Jason grinned. "Come on Alex, get in. I don't want to go without you."

Alex could see her younger brother was determined and she knew she better not let him go without her there to keep him out of trouble. Now she really wished Charlie was back from visiting with his mother.

She got into the boat. "Okay you guys, but we stay in the boats. There'll be no going on his property. Are we clear?" She looked at them authoritatively.

"Yeah, yeah," they murmured in unified assent.

The boys started the motors and they were off.

Alex noticed the water was smoother and the air was calmer than when she and Charlie had canoed across yesterday. With the motor boats they reached the other side quickly, shut of the motors, took out the fishing rods and waited.

And waited.

And waited some more.

The fish weren't biting. There was no sign of Mr. Hawthorn. There were no gigantic prehistoric turtles floating around.

"This is pretty boring," Leeanna announced at last.

"Wow, welcome to real life sleuthing," Andrew announced. "Detectives have to do a lot of waiting in order to actually discover something significant. At least that's what my Dad always says."

"Wish I brought a book to read, or something to write in," Alex mused.

"I wonder if I'd get wi-fi out here if I'd brought my laptop," Pete wondered.

"Probably not," Alex commiserated.

Suddenly a motor boat sped towards them. The driver, an elderly lady, regarded them intently as she approached, and next to her in the passenger seat, proudly sat a brown and white fluffy dog, his fur flying in the wind.

It was the lady Charlie and Alex had seen on the dock of the property next to Mr. Hawthorn's.

She cut the engine, letting her beautiful white fiberglass boat drift towards them.

"Hi kids," she called in a friendly voice. "I'm Ms. Reilly."

Her boat was only meters away now.

"You shouldn't be this far from camp you know. Mr. Evans would not be happy that you're all the way over here," Ms. Reilly added.

"You are the lady that helps out in the camp kitchen," Alex blurted.

Ms. Reilly smiled. "Yes, I am. Come on guys. Follow me. You should not be near this property. The man who lives here doesn't want to see anyone."

Her motor propelled her boat out into the lake and she waited for them to follow her.

Feeling they really had no choice for fear she'd rat them out to Mr. Evans, they decided the best course of action was to do as she recommended.

They slowly followed Ms. Reilly over to her property. Everyone met at her rather large dock, where she had a table and several lawn chairs set out. The table held a bright yellow tray containing a plate of cookies, a large pitcher of lemonade and a bunch of glasses.

She tied her boat to the dock and motioned to the kids to do the same. Wordlessly they did as they were instructed and in a matter of moments they were all seated in lawn chairs in the brilliant sunshine.

"Oatmeal chocolate chip," she waved her hand towards the cookies. "I made them about an hour ago."

"Looks like you were expecting us," Andrew commented.

"Well, I did see you heading over there and rather than see you get into trouble, I thought I'd make you a better offer," Ms. Reilly smiled.

The kids dug in after Alex gave them an affirming nod. After all, they all knew Ms. Reilly was an excellent cook.

"This is Puck," she pointed to the grinning dog by her side. "I named him after Puck in A Midsummer Night's Dream. I'm kind of a Shakespeare fan," she explained.

The kids smiled at one another. This was certainly better than waiting for that horrible Mr. Hawthorn to descend upon them.

They chatted with the elderly cook for awhile, who seemed happy to have the company and it wasn't long before the plate of cookies and the jug of lemonade were both empty. They told her stories about their time at camp, how they were excited to go to high school and that soon Alex would be the last of the gang to be turning fourteen.

"Well, except for me of course," Jason grinned proudly. "I'm hanging out with the big kids."

"Yeah, he's kinda like our mascot," Andrew joked and roughed up Jason's hair with a few back handed swipes of his hand.

Jason did not look amused but handled it with dignity.

"Is it true that you sold a big portion of your land to Mr. Evans' parents so the camp could be built?" Alex questioned.

"Yes," Ms. Reilly said simply.

Puck, his head hanging over the edge of the dock, was growling at something.

The kids laughed good humouredly at Jason's reaction. Ms. Reilly smiled and turned to see what Puck was up to.

She pushed her chair back and bent down to try to see what Puck was looking at. She gently touched the top of his head and stroked it lovingly.

"What is it boy?" she whispered.

The dog growled again, more agitatedly this time. Alex went to look and the others got up from their chairs to see what was going on, on that side of the dock.

230

Puck and all the humans jumped back as something large, hard shelled and ancient emerged from the lake.

It was a gigantic turtle!

CHAPTER TWENTY NINE

There was screaming and dog barking and general pandemonium until Ms. Reilly reached down and touched the turtle with her bare hands.

Everyone silently stared, stunned.

"A little joke," she grinned up at them. "I think someone's having a little fun at our expense." A hollow sound came up from the shell as she pounded on the turtle's exterior.

"A fake?" Leeanna exclaimed incredulously.

"Apparently," Ms. Reilly remarked as she stood up and wiped her wet hands on her jeans.

"Who would do such a thing?" Jason was blown away.

Ms. Reilly looked at each of the children in turn and seemed to consider very carefully what she would say next. Then at last she said, "I think you guys had better get back to camp before someone thinks you've come in harm's way."

Quickly, she encouraged everyone to get back in the boats and head across the water. As she stood waving to them on the dock, with Puck at her side, Alex wondered why Ms. Reilly suddenly seemed in such a hurry to get rid of them.

They clamored out of the boats at the camp's docks, speechless with surprise.

"What the heck was that all about?" Andrew wondered.

"Who would make a fake turtle and what was it doing there? It certainly didn't make Puck a happy puppy," Jason was flabbergasted and furious at the same time.

Pete hadn't said a word all the way cross the lake. That usually meant he was thinking. That usually meant he was thinking about something really, really big.

"Guys," he said at last as they all stood on the dock staring at him. "I think that old man made that stupid fake turtle."

"What?" Leeanna blurted.

"I think he made that turtle to feed the myth so people would stay away from his property," he explained. "Did you see it though? That bad plastic, crappy paint and the dumb old rope on the end he must have used to haul it in."

"How do you think it ended up by Ms. Reilly's dock?" Jason asked.

"Oh, the wind probably just blew it over," Alex said, remembering how the canoe had also ended up there.

An evil smile spread itself across Pete's face.

"I'm going to beat that old man at his own game. I'm going to make an awesome remote control turtle and freak that guy out. I'm going to give him a taste of his own medicine."

"Awesome," Jason exploded with glee.

"So cool!" Leeanna uttered.

"Not so cool," Alex said suddenly. "What if you're right and the old man fabricated that fake turtle to keep people away. He has a right to his privacy. What if that stuff about his son dying is actually true and he just can't deal with seeing anybody. Don't you think it's better to leave him alone?"

They all looked at Alex and then burst out laughing.

"Sorry Alex, it's just way too much fun messing with this old guy," Andrew said. "Besides it's just a little practical joke. He's just going to be surprised when a turtle he doesn't recognize shows up on his beach uninvited."

The other kids laughed all the way to their cabins as Alex stood on the dock.

After awhile she sat on the edge and dangled her feet into the water. She watched some ducks floating by and thought of the time Charlie had almost hit a family of ducks during his first wind surfing lesson. She smiled to herself. She missed Charlie.

Some of the younger kids came to the dock and she helped them rip up bread to feed the little feathered friends. The young campers were happy to tell Alex all about their day's adventures at camp.

They spotted minnows flitting about in the shallow water and watched long legged bugs stride across the surface of the lake. The bull rushes swayed in the soft evening breeze.

At last it was time to head to the dining hall for dinner. The little kids, tummies growling, took off as Alex indulged herself in a few more minutes of peaceful tranquility.

As she looked across the lake, she found herself thinking about Mr. Hawthorn. He seemed so alone, so cut off from everyone who must have cared about him. Would he really choose to live like this just because his son died so long ago?

She heard angry footsteps thumping across the dock.

She turned to look at who was coming towards her. It was Charlie, his blue eyes blazing, fury clouding his face.

He reached down and swiftly pulled her to her feet.

Wide eyed, she stared up at him.

"What the hell do you think you're doing?" he uttered, with barely concealed rage.

CHAPTER THIRTY

"Charlie, what's wrong?" Alex stammered.

She had never seen him so angry, so unlike himself.

"I just got back, and I find out from the guys that you went over to Hawthorn's place again – without me."

"Look Charlie, I can explain –" Alex began soothingly.

"Alex!! What were you thinking? The guy's got a shot gun for God's sake and that devil dog of his makes the Hound of the Baskervilles look like freakin' Scooby Doo. I can't protect you if I'm not even there."

He was shaking, his breathing coming in ragged gasps and he looked as though he might cry. Alex stared incredulously into his eyes, sorry to see him so distraught, and took his face into her hands.

"I'm fine. I never set foot on his property. Everything's okay," she whispered gently.

"Oh God, Alex," he murmured desperately, "If anything bad happened to you, I would seriously lose it."

She wrapped her arms around his neck and they held each other for a long time.

After awhile she could feel that his breathing had returned to normal and that he seemed calmer.

"Did you have a nice visit with your mother?"

"Yeah, she's good," he said contentedly, and grinned at her.

"What?

"She said I had a happy glow about me."

"Really?" Alex smirked.

"So she had a great time teasing me about you."

"So she's cool, with us?"

"She's always adored you Alex."

Alex smiled thoughtfully.

Charlie looked down into her face. "What are you thinking?"

"I was thinking about how furious you were and –"

"And now you're thinking I'm an absolute lunatic. Please, please, please don't hold it against me. I was just really, really scared something horrible could happen and –"

"Charlie," she interrupted. "What I'm thinking is that fear and pain can cause strange and powerful reactions. Maybe that's why Mr. Hawthorn is the way he is. Maybe he's so full of fear and pain that he can't move forward from his son's death. Maybe that's why he shut himself off from everyone."

Charlie smiled indulgently at her. "I recognize that look on your face. You are formulating a plan."

"I think we should reach out to him. I think we should offer our friendship."

"You really are the craziest girl on the planet," he grinned.

"Will you help me?"

"Sure, spoken like the true lunatic I must be. But we have to talk terms. This plan of yours in no way involves getting up close and personal with that tooth factory of a dog."

"What's the matter Shaggy, are you afraid of a big bear hug from Scooby Doo?" she teased.

"First of all that killing machine is not a Great Dane, it's a Rottweiler and second of all, you're so not funny."

"Yes, I am."

He put his arm around her and together they walked up to the dining hall for dinner.

239

At breakfast the next morning Pete and Jason could not stop talking about their remote control turtle. Pete had hitched a ride into town with Charlie's mother, picked up a few supplies and made the fifteen minute ride back with Mrs. Clifton. They'd had a nice talk about how much fun all the kids were having at camp.

Alex went to the kitchen after breakfast to begin step one of her plan. She didn't want anything to do with the remote control turtle scheme.

"Good morning Ms. Reilly," she began. "I was wondering if you might be able to help me with something."

"Of course, dear," she returned as she stacked the dishwasher with some morning dishes.

"Well, since you make awesome cookies, I was wondering if I could help you make a batch and leave them in a little container on Mr. Hawthorn's dock."

Ms. Reilly stopped what she was doing and regarded Alex carefully.

"Why would you want to do that dear?"

"Well, I think maybe he could be lonely and sad. Maybe he could use some friends and who better than a bunch of crazy kids like me and my buddies?"

Ms. Reilly laughed and then checked herself. "Oh, I don't know –"

"What harm could it do, really?" Alex pleaded.

Leeanna entered the kitchen. "And while we're at it, I'm going to kill that dog of his with kindness by making it some homemade doggy treats. My Dad and I make them all the time for our Yorkies."

Ms. Reilly considered both girls' smiling, pleading faces and gave in, in the end.

Later that morning Alex talked Charlie into taking the little fishing boat out with her and depositing the container of cookies and the little bag of dog treats on Mr. Hawthorn's dock.

Charlie booked it out of there as fast as that motor would go, shaking his head in disbelief at Alex's crazy ideas.

At lunch Alex approached Mr. Evans as he sat with some of the other counselors and asked him if they could invite Mr. Hawthorn to join the camp for the next campfire and stories evening.

"Well, Alex, I'm not sure he'd be interested. He's pretty reclusive," Mr. Evans began.

"I don't think there'd be any harm in asking him," Alex persisted.

"I don't think that's such a good idea," Ms. Reilly interjected as she placed slices of apple pie out on the tables.

Alex turned and looked at her with wide eyes, surprised at her reluctance.

"Well, it's one thing to leave an old man a container of cookies –" Ms. Reilly began.

"Highly superior cookies, I might add," Alex interjected good humouredly.

"Thank you dear," Ms. Reilly acknowledged. "But it's quite another thing to invite someone who wants nothing to do with people to sit around a campfire with a camp full of kids. It may be too much. That's just my opinion," she stated and returned to the kitchen.

Slowly, people began leaving the dining hall to go about their afternoon activities. As Mr. Evans headed for the door, Alex followed.

"What do you think Mr. E?" she reiterated. "Can I give it a shot and invite the old guy?"

Mr. Evans paused, thought a moment, then shrugged his shoulders and said, "I guess there's no harm in trying. But I have to say, Ms. Reilly's right. Any time I've seen him over the years, he's always been a tough customer. But I see you're on a mission Alex, so go ahead."

"Thanks Mr. Evans," she exclaimed gleefully.

"Good luck," he added somewhat ominously as he left the hall.

Later that night as the campers gathered to watch a movie and gobble up popcorn in the main hall, Alex and Charlie noticed Pete and Jason did not come to see the movie. Andrew sat with Erica a little too far away for them to talk to him. Leeanna came in late and squeezed in next to Alex.

"Where's Pete and Jason?" Alex whispered.

"They're working on the turtle. They're obsessed. It's like they're making a movie prop that's going to horrify theatre-goers everywhere," she grinned.

"I'm really not happy about that stupid turtle," Alex hissed. "I don't think they should try to scare the old guy."

"Oh, they're just going to have some childish fun. I don't think they mean to hurt anyone," Leeanna assured her.

"Ah, but when one creates a monster, one cannot always control the havoc that monster creates. Just ask Victor Frankenstein."

CHAPTER THIRTY ONE

The next morning at breakfast Charlie and Alex sat with Andrew.

"Hey dude," Charlie began. "How's it going with the archery?"

"Pretty good actually," Andrew grinned. "I've been practicing a lot."

"Yeah, that's because you met that hot redhead at the archery targets," Charlie teased.

"Well maybe that has something to do with it," Andrew admitted.

"She's really nice," Alex added.

"We need you to help us with a little job," Charlie said directly.

"Ah ha," Andrew murmured as he buttered his hot, fresh cranberry muffin.

"Charlie and I want you to come with us in the motor boat over to Mr. Hawthorn's place. Bring your bow and arrow," said Alex.

Andrew's mouth dropped open and a piece of muffin fell out. "You want me to shoot the old guy?" he whispered, horrified.

Alex and Charlie burst out laughing as Andrew embarrassedly collected the escaped piece of muffin.

"No, oh God, no," Alex explained, lowering her voice to a whisper. "We want to wrap a little note around the arrow, secure it to the shaft with a piece of string and fire it at one of his trees near the dock so he'll find it and get our message."

"Oh, that makes total sense because we don't have telephones, post offices or email to communicate out here in the wilderness," Andrew returned sarcastically.

"Will you do it?" Alex asked.

Andrew thought about it for a moment.

He shrugged his shoulders. "Sure, whatever."

"Great, we'll meet you on the dock in fifteen minutes," Alex said, leaving the table abruptly.

Andrew turned to Charlie.

"So another crazy idea brought to you by Alexandria Lawrence," Andrew joked.

"Thanks man, it really means a lot to her to try to help this old fellow. She feels really sad for him, what with his son dying and all."

"Yeah, sure. No problem. I totally get it. Alex has a soft spot for outcasts who don't seem to fit in," Andrew

246

teasingly glared at Charlie who returned a disbelieving stare.

Andrew laughed good naturedly. "I'm just messing with you dude. Let's go."

It wasn't long before the three of them sat in the little fishing boat and puttered across the lake. Alex busily wrapped the little note around one of the arrow's shafts and secured it with a tiny piece of string. Andrew had brought a second arrow just in case.

"What does the note say anyway?" Andrew asked.

"We're just inviting him to tomorrow night's campfire and storytelling time," Alex explained as she handed Andrew the arrow.

They neared the shore and Charlie cut the engine. Andrew picked up the bow, secured the arrow and began setting up the shot. Alex quietly pointed to a tree she thought would make a suitable target and carefully switched places with Andrew so he would be in the front of the boat.

He pulled back the bow-string, aimed and released the arrow.

It hit the tree, embedding the arrow tip in the rough bark. The shaft wobbled back and forth for a few seconds and then held firm.

"Nicely done," Alex exclaimed.

"Yeah, pretty impressive," Charlie said admiringly.

Andrew smiled with satisfaction as Charlie started the motor and turned them around.

They dropped Andrew at the dock minutes later.

"Thanks for helping us out," Alex said as he stepped out of the boat.

"No problem. It was actually kind of fun. Do you think he'll accept the invitation?"

"I hope so," Alex returned.

"See you guys later. Happy Birthday, Alex!" Andrew added.

"Wow! Thanks. You remembered?"

"It's the same day every year," Andrew grinned as he headed down the dock.

"Hey Alex, let's go for a little spin around the lake," Charlie suggested as he backed the boat up.

"Sounds great."

Charlie took them over to a peaceful section of the lake near Ms. Reilly's property. It was quiet and the water, filled with water lilies, was a calm, deep green.

Alex took a deep breath of fresh air and regarded her surroundings.

"I can totally see why those Group of Seven painters spent so much time in the Canadian north. There is such a serene and rugged beauty up here."

Charlie smiled and took a little box out of his pocket.

"Happy Birthday," he said softly, nervously opening up the little green box and turning the open side towards her.

On a bed of black velvet lay a stunning silver rope chain. Hanging from it was an intricately detailed silver pendant in the shape of an antique Victorian key.

She looked into his face, speechless.

"I thought of you the moment I saw it," he began.

"When did you --?"

"When I had lunch with Mom, we did a little shopping. She helped me pick a really solid chain so you wouldn't lose it easily. You know when you're out solving mysteries or having other adventures. The antique key reminded me of you because you love old things especially stories from the 1800s, and you're always looking for the key to solve a mystery."

"It's so beautiful. Thank you, Charlie. Will you help me put it on?"

He reached into the box and removed the necklace as Alex leaned forward.

"Wow, you're assuming I have the coordination and talent it takes to pull this off," he joked as he awkwardly tried to clasp the chain around her neck.

"There," he said with satisfaction. "Ta da!!"

Alex kissed him.

"It's the best birthday present ever," she uttered.

And then they could hear Pete and Jason zooming across the lake in a little fishing boat, squealing and laughing with delight.

Charlie and Alex turned surprised faces in the direction of the noise and watched as the boys' plan unfolded.

Pete stopped the engine in the middle of the lake and Jason helped him haul something out of the boat and into the water. It was their remote control turtle. It only took seconds before they could see it was moving towards

Mr. Hawthorn's dock as Pete controlled its actions with a device he held in his hands. Those evil scientist brats, Alex thought to herself. Mr. Hawthorn will never take their offer of friendship if he discovers those two and their stupid turtle.

Just then, the big black barking Rottweiler rounded the crest of the hill.

CHAPTER THIRTY TWO

The dog bolted down the hill and came to a skidding stop as the turtle swam around the front of the dock.

Pete and Jason took one startled look at the ferocious beast barking at their turtle, dripping saliva in its fury, its muscles taut and ready to jump into the water, when Mr. Hawthorn came running down the hill in the dog's wake.

"Stay Sikes," he ordered the dog, and Sikes obediently sat on the edge of the dock, his body shaking with desire to go at the thing in the water, his eyes pleading with his master to let him.

"What did you find there, buddy?" Mr. Hawthorn asked gently.

Sikes whined and fidgeted as Mr. Hawthorn followed his gaze and stared into the water.

And then he saw it.

The old man's eyes widened with mingled surprise and fear.

"Sikes come," he directed and the man and his dog disappeared up the hill.

Pete quickly radioed the turtle back to their boat, Jason helped him haul it over the edge and they sped off back to camp, laughing hysterically all the way.

Charlie and Alex looked at one another.

"He'll never accept our invitation now," Alex groaned.

Charlie started the motor and they headed back to camp.

At dinner time Alex noticed that Ms. Reilly wasn't in the kitchen.

Mr. Evans asked them if they'd seen any turtles lately and Pete and Jason could hardly keep themselves from exploding with laughter. Alex just scowled at them and mumbled something about them turning to the Dark Side.

As the campers assembled around the camp fire, people were chatting excitedly about their day's activities.

Charlie noticed Alex was unusually quiet and as he put his lawn chair next to hers, he gently took her hand. She gave him a weak smile and he squeezed her hand encouragingly.

"The night's not over yet," he whispered. "He might still come."

The marshmallows went around and people told stories. They laughed and joked.

Leeanna sat on Alex's other side.

"That's a pretty necklace Alex. Where did you get that?" she smiled coyly.

"It's my birthday present from Charlie," she said proudly.

"Oooh," Leeanna teased.

Alex laughed.

Suddenly everyone was singing Happy Birthday as Mr. Evans joined the circle carrying a big cake with candles on it. Fourteen to be exact.

"Happy Birthday," he grinned. "I thought everyone might like to dig into a cake and your birthday gave me just the excuse I needed."

The kids all cheered.

"Ms. Reilly made it," Mr. Evans explained as Alex blew out the candles.

"Wow, that means it's going to be delicious. For a second there I thought you'd made it," Charlie joked.

Mr. Evans grinned. "You are a funny guy, Charlie," he quipped with mock sarcasm.

Leeanna and Pete helped pass out pieces of cake to everyone.

That was when Mr. Hawthorn and his dog appeared. Everyone stopped and stared, forks full of cake arrested between plates and mouths, eyes wide in disbelief.

Mr. Hawthorn, clean shaven, hair cut and brushed wore a tentative smile that could not hide his nervousness. Next to him stood Ms. Reilly and Puck, her arm looped through the old man's as she gently and encouragingly guided him to a chair around the fire.

"Welcome," Mr. Evans stammered incredulously. "Join us, please."

They sat down and both dogs lay quietly in front of their masters.

Alex could hardly believe the transformation from a ragged, wild, furious, terror to this quiet well groomed man sitting by the fire surrounded by a bunch of kids. He didn't even look so old any more.

"We're so glad you came," Alex found her voice at last.

"Roman was very happy to receive your invitation," Ms. Reilly began. "He agreed it was time for a change. He thinks he's ready to move forward after the death of our son, William."

"Let me explain Juliette," Mr. Hawthorn said softly and took a deep breath before he began. "Many years ago, when William was killed, everything fell apart for me. My wife and I divorced, we split up our land and I isolated myself from the world. I guess I was kind of like Miss Havisham in Great Expectations."

The children all looked confused.

Ms. Reilly continued. "After the divorce I tried to make a new life for myself. I dropped my married name, Hawthorn, and went back to my maiden name, Reilly. I sold some of my land so this camp could be built," continued Ms. Reilly. "I came to help out in the kitchen. It made me feel better to have someone to cook for and to be surrounded by children's laughter. Everyone handles grief in their own way."

"I'd like to thank the kids who reached out and tried to make a difference," Mr. Hawthorn said appreciatively.

"Alex would be the leader in that department," Charlie spoke up.

Mr. Hawthorn got up from his chair and shook Alex's hand with dignity and grace. "Thank you," he said simply.

Alex smiled as warm joy spread through her. "You're very welcome Mr. Hawthorn."

"Please, call me Roman."

"So, Roman and Juliette," Charlie chuckled.

"Well Charlie," Ms. Reilly beamed. "You would not be the first person to make the Romeo and Juliette joke. Remember my dog's name is Puck and our son was William."

"As in Shakespeare," Leeanna put in. "And by the way, I could use a little help here."

Sikes' head was practically in Leeanna's lap as he nuzzled her lovingly.

"Ah, you must be the doggy treat chef," Roman observed. "Your scent would have been all over those goodies, so Sikes adores you now. Sorry," he apologized as he gently led his dog back to his seat.

Leeanna giggled. "No problem. Is Sikes from Shakespeare too?"

"Dickens, Oliver Twist," he explained. "I was a Victorian literature professor before I retired. Dickens is my favourite."

Then spontaneously he went around to gallantly shake everyone's hand, thank them for coming to camp and express his sincere hope that everyone was having a good time. Some of the kids were not exactly sure what was going on, but filled with cake and marshmallows they unquestioningly accepted the happiness that ensued.

When everyone was seated around the camp fire again, Mr. Hawthorn made an amazing announcement. "Today I saw a huge turtle on my side of the lake."

Pete and Jason froze.

"Now I'm going to admit I made my own little model turtle to keep people away over the years, but the turtle I saw today was spectacular. By the time Sikes and I could get back with my camera it was, of course, gone."

"Spit it out Pete, Jason," Alex demanded.

"Ah, Mr. Hawthorn, Roman," Pete smiled nervously. "That turtle was our handy work I'm afraid," he admitted, pointing to himself and Jason. "We made a remote control turtle, to one-up you on the fake turtle we found. It was supposed to be a little harmless fun."

"We're sorry," Jason added weakly.

Roman and Juliette laughed heartily.

"Wow, I'm really impressed you guys went to so much trouble to get my attention," Roman responded.

"Just think," Juliette added. "While I was over at Roman's place this afternoon trying to make him understand how much you kids cared, he would have missed that grand turtle if it weren't for Sikes." She petted the Rottweiler affectionately on the head.

Roman smiled. "I'd like to talk to you later Mr. Evans about setting up a little scholarship in William's name for children whose families might benefit from a little help in order to send their children to camp. Everyone deserves a little of this." He looked around at all the smiling faces.

"That sounds wonderful," Mr. Evans exclaimed.

"And I intend to still look for those mythical turtles," Roman added.

"There are sightings back into the 1870s according to local articles, so there has to be some truth in the legend," Jason added eagerly, still harbouring the hope that he too would see one.

"Actually, that might just be because the local newspaper went into print in the 1800s. Local Native legends tell an ancient myth about the Great Turtle who is the beginning of the creation of the first land on this watery globe. Look it up. The turtle is an important creature."

"Would you like some birthday cake?" Alex asked.

"Don't mind if I do," Roman smiled as he accepted the cake.

It was the first birthday party he had been to in eighteen years.

CHAPTER THIRTY THREE

It was a peaceful dawn.

Alex came to the beach seeking inspiration for a new story to write.

Slowly other campers awoke and began heading to the dining hall for breakfast.

She was content. Camp would soon be over for the summer, but she would be taking awesome memories home with her, and who knows, maybe they could come back again next summer. Soon the adventures of high school awaited Alex and her friends.

She walked quietly along the sandy edge of the water.

And then she saw it.

It was an impression in the sand. A large oval impression made by a heavy creature. On each side of the oval, top and bottom, were two footprints that looked like they had been created by a gigantic turtle.

ABOUT THE AUTHOR

Andrea Hertach has been an elementary school teacher for more than 27 years. The Monster Mob is her second children's novel following on the heals of Swamped, a novel about a little girl who tries to save an eco-system. Andrea has been published in various magazines and industry periodicals, receiving a writer's award for her contribution to VOICE Magazine. She has her Masters degree in Education and enjoys sharing mysteries with her family, friends and students. She has been spotted on Halloween night dressed as Sherlock Holmes walking the Hounds of the Baskervilles, her two Shetland Sheepdogs.

CPSIA information can be obtained
at www.ICGtesting.com
Printed in the USA
LVOW04s0250220216
476111LV00030B/506/P